A
FRIEND
IN THE
GLASS

AN AUDEN & O'CALLAGHAN MYSTERY

GREGORY ASHE
C.S. POE

A Friend in the Glass

Published by Emporium Press
https://www.cspoe.com
contact@cspoe.com

Cover Art by Reese Dante
Cover content is for illustrative purposes only and any person depicted on the cover is a model.

Copyedited by Andrea Zimmerman
Proofread by Lyrical Lines

Published 2024.
Printed in the United States of America

Trade Paperback ISBN: 978-1-952133-55-8
Digital eBook ISBN: 978-1-952133-54-1

The best mirror is an old friend.

CHAPTER
ONE

At 4:32 p.m. Rufus O'Callaghan was shadowing a redheaded dipshit with a Dr. Robotnik mustache, who the NYPD referred to as Chad (last name unknown), while he strolled through Union Square's Greenmarket. The guy was acting like he didn't have a care in the world. And maybe he didn't. Rufus just found it odd that a mover in the underground drug trade, whose latest fentanyl-laced coke sales in the city had caused the deaths of at least five people—and so had piqued the interest of the cops—was stopping to literally smell the flowers.

Rufus stood behind the parked van of one of the numerous upstate farmers, its advertising decal simple and to the point: GOAT.

Goat *what*, though? Goat milk? Goat cheese? Fuck, maybe they sold actual live goats, and some dumbass city folk were trying to decide if a barnyard animal would qualify under the terms and conditions of their lease as a twenty-pound pet.

Rufus tugged his sunglasses off and slid the plastic frames into his pocket. The sun set so fucking early in December. Not even five o'clock and it was dark. Rufus's therapist thought he needed a SAD lamp.

And he probably did. But Rufus wasn't about to dump two hundred bucks on a fancy light bulb. Even with a confirmed diagnosis of clinical depression, panic disorder, and PTSD (because Rufus had had a traumatic childhood, in case he wasn't aware), he still wasn't going to spend over a month's worth of food money on a lamp. Especially when Detective Erik Weaver frowned upon Rufus pocketing bodega snacks.

Rufus hunched his shoulders as a gale straight out of the Arctic blew through the Square. Dead leaves, litter, and loose business cards from tabletops were swept up in a little urban twister, only to be deposited a dozen feet away in the frozen, dirty snowbanks lining the sidewalks and streets. Rufus had picked up a new, *used*, jean jacket from a closet-sized shop on St. Marks after the previous one had been sacrificed to sop up Sam's blood from a knife wound. This one fit perfectly in the shoulders and arms, even came with a Dead Kennedys pin on the collar, but despite also wearing a black hoodie underneath, two pairs of socks, and his faithful beanie, Rufus was still cold as hell.

All height and no mass.

Chad waved off a florist's attempt to sell him a potted chrysanthemum and finally started walking uptown again.

"Thank fuck," Rufus mumbled as he left the GOAT-mobile. He followed at a distance of about half a block—and was mindful that rush hour was descending upon

Midtown—because in a neighborhood where people had money, Chad's black Canada Goose jacket was starting to blend in with all the others.

A construction worker threw open a site access door in front of Rufus, nearly braining him. Ignoring the redhead, he barked orders toward the street in Spanish, and two more guys in reflective vests and hardhats maneuvered a huge plate of glass across the sidewalk, cutting the foot traffic like a hot knife through butter. Rufus dodged around the farthest guy, swearing all the while.

Chad had vanished so suddenly, he could have been a victim in an episode of *Unsolved Mysteries*.

Rufus jogged the rest of the block, jumped a river of brown slush on the corner that the street gutters were unable to keep up with after the amount of snow that'd recently fallen, and caught Chad entering a bodega on the corner of Twenty-First and Third. Rufus followed.

The thing about Chad was that the cops had been champing at the bit for him for a while, but there was never enough evidence to prove he'd been the one actually dealing. It was always a "he said, she said" kind of situation. But after those folks had dropped dead, pressure mounted to catch Chad in the act of selling his fentanyl-laced garbage. The NYPD had been scoping out Port Authority, certain Chad would be making his trade-offs there, considering it was such a hotspot for hard drugs in the city, but when they had nothing to show for their time and money, CIs had been called. Specifically, Rufus had been called. And while it wasn't a particularly thrilling assignment, he knew that the cops—bless their hearts— were playing a game of Marco Polo with a brick wall. So he'd agreed to the job, and within two days, had found Chad.

The bell over the door chimed as Rufus stepped inside the bodega. He wandered down the aisle of processed snack foods opposite the drink coolers. He grabbed a bag of Takis, tore it open, and pulled a few hot sticks out to eat while moseying to the counter. Chad stood there, pretending to read one of the few subway rags still making its money from print editions. He murmured opinions on the headlines to the man behind the counter.

The guy manning the register, his attention mostly on Chad, glanced at Rufus long enough to say, "Buck fifty."

"Can I get one of those scratch-offs too?" Rufus pointed to the roll of tickets hanging from the wall at the man's back. "The two-dollar game." He slid a few dollars across the counter, accepted the lotto ticket, and moved back several steps to a refrigerated deli case. Leaning against the rounded glass, Rufus pocketed the Takis and then dug out a quarter and his burner phone. He turned on the screen and a text message from an unknown number immediately popped up.

GENTLE PATRIOT! JEN NASTA HERE. I'M RUNNING FOR REELECTION, AND I NEED YOUR HELP. ARE YOU REGISTERED TO VOTE IN THE COMING NEW YEAR?

Rufus dismissed the message and tapped the camera app.

Another text notification appeared.

IT'S YOUR AMERICAN DUTY!

And another.

MAKE YOUR VOICE HEARD!

"Fucking Christ," Rufus whispered.

TYPE Y FOR YES AND N FOR NO. TEXT MESSAGE RATES MAY APPLY.

Rufus swallowed a growl, tapped *Y* to get the voting bot off his goddamn back, then positioned himself in such a way that while scratching the lotto ticket with the edge of his quarter, he could rest the phone in the bend of his elbow and snap photos of Chad dealing coke to the bodega guy who had a face full of acne scars. Rufus *tap*, *tap*, *tap*ped the phone's screen, picture after picture with the location, date, and time metadata turned on, catching Chad not so discreetly passing drugs in a fumbling handshake.

HELP US MAKE AMERICA SAFE AGAIN BY DONATING NOW.

"Fuck," Rufus said, this time loud enough that he saw Chad, from the corner of his eye, turn to look. So Rufus blurted out, "I didn't win."

Chad said something that sounded suspiciously like "Dumbass fag" before he saw himself out.

Rufus tore the lotto ticket into a few pieces and shoved the confetti into his jacket pocket. As he passed the cashier, he said, "Have a good night."

"Whatever."

When Rufus stepped outside, Chad had already disappeared into the evening crowds. Opening a blank text message, he put in Erik's number from memory, dropped a map with a pin, then flooded the detective with the still photos he'd taken.

Erik responded within a minute—a thumbs-up emoji.

Having earned his paycheck for the week, Rufus put his hands into his pockets, about-faced, and started the long walk home.

CHAPTER
TWO

The honking on the street below never stopped. Sirens, twenty-four / seven. The radiators were always clanking, the pipes rattling, the boiler occasionally booming, the whole building like a pressure cooker about to blow. *Jeopardy!* at four from the apartment below. Duran Duran from the shit-for-brains next door, at any hour of the day, whenever the fancy struck him. Which begged the question, in Sam Auden's humble opinion, of who the fuck had ever been struck by the need to listen to Duran Duran.

Sam thought maybe he needed to get out of the house.

Well, house was a generous term. He needed to get out of the apartment. The studio apartment. The small studio apartment. The tiny little fuckhole, if he was being technical, that in the greatest city in the world apparently was considered a reasonably sized space to live.

Ok, he thought. Maybe he needed to get out of the city.

Instead, he did the dishes, which were left over from the spaghetti Rufus had thrown together the night before and which were starting to smell. Nobody else might have noticed yet, but he did, and it was worse in the cramped quarters. He soaked the plates and the pot. He scrubbed the hardened red sauce with the brush. Then he went for the sponge. When that didn't work, he banged the pot on the stainless-steel rim of the sink and muttered, "Fuck this shit."

Scummy water, greasy with olive oil and speckled with tomato pulp, splashed across his shirt and jeans. The combination of the wet warmth and the smell sent him into overload. It wasn't a panic attack, but in some ways, it felt like one. Racing heartbeat. Hyperfocused sensory awareness. The need to crawl out of his fucking skin, that was another good one. He clutched the countertop, knuckles blanching, and focused on his breathing until he felt a little less fried and a little more human.

The fluoxetine had been helping. But this was the city that never shut its fucking eyes, never gave a guy a break.

Stripping out of the soiled clothes, Sam told himself the meds did help. Still helped. He showered with Dr. Bronner's Pure Castile Bar Soap, Baby Unscented, which sounded in his head like something a traveling medicine man might hawk from the back of a stagecoach. Lukewarm water. Pressure so low it might as well have been dripping out of the showerhead. He dried off with the towel that was perpetually damp and changed into clean clothes: jeans, a white tee inside out, socks inside out, boots.

The hamper was starting to smell too, so he added the clothes that were the victim of spaghetti water and carried the whole load downstairs to the laundry in the basement. He only had enough quarters for one load, so he packed the drum tight. Then he realized he'd forgotten the soap; he was still used to laundromats where he could buy it when he needed to. He left the clothes in the washer and hiked up the five flights of stairs. He got the detergent, some sort of free and clear gentle stuff that Rufus had found on sale, and took it back downstairs.

The washer was now chugging dourly. The clothes he'd loaded lay in a heap on the floor. He opened the washer's lid, saw the Under Armour shorts and the Nike tanks, and decided that he was going to murder Gym Bro, 2A.

Some big-hearted super had, at some point, added a plastic chair to the laundry room. It had a wonky leg, and the one time Sam had sat in it, it had made a noise that had given Rufus something to laugh about for a week. Sam dropped into the seat, ignoring the metallic squeal of protest. He studied the laundry room. The two-tube fluorescent strip overhead had a cracked acrylic panel, and one of the tubes fluttered intermittently. On the far wall, Mrs. Costello had tacked red-foil letters that spelled out MERRY CHRISTMAS AND HAPPY HOLIDAYS. The artificial perfume of 2A's detergent was underlain by the smell of perpetual moisture—something between mildew and wet wool, which Sam suspected was coming from the floor drain. The washer's motor groaned as the drum spun. A pipe clanked. He'd heard fags burned in hell. Nobody had warned him about winters in Manhattan.

Rufus would be home. Eventually. If whatever he was doing—snooping, snitching, digging up dirt he could sell to Erik Weaver, his handler at the NYPD—didn't keep him out late. And that was good. That was great. They'd talk. And Sam would ask about Rufus's day. But then Rufus might want to go out for pizza. Or he'd want to see the library. Or it was the free day at a museum he hadn't visited recently. And that would mean the subway, the smell of piss, the heat of bodies and trapped air, the stink of sweat trapped in winter coats. Or the sidewalk, the patterns Sam couldn't suss out, taxis cutting through crosswalks, the flash of electric signage.

He closed his eyes. He pictured Arkansas. Outside Eureka Springs. April. The bluegrass coming back to life. The sound of a semi pounding past, the silent skitter of the gravel on the shoulder. A wall of air pressing against his cheek. Cow dung. The cottonwoods like old women bending over a creek far off in the pasture. The soundtrack was Howlin' Wolf, and he was howling right after that smokestack lightning hit. Why don't you hear. Why don't you hear me cryin'.

That was when the chair gave out, and Sam landed on the leg where he'd been shot two months before.

CHAPTER
THREE

The phone call came the next morning while they were still in bed.

Sam fumbled through the strata of blankets, trying to find the source of the buzzing, eyes still bleary with sleep. "God damn it. If this is Weaver again because you two got your signals crossed...."

Rufus responded with what sounded like a snore.

By the time Sam's fingers closed around the phone, it was on the fourth ring. He blinked at the unknown number and let the call go to voicemail. He played the message a moment later.

The woman had obviously started speaking too soon, and the words were clipped with hurry. "—Shareed Baker, and I have information I think you'll be interested in. I'm going to call you again in five minutes. If you're smart, you'll pick up."

As if Rufus had only just registered Sam's comment, he asked, "Why'd Erik call you?"

"Not Erik," Sam said. He dropped down on the pillow and scratched Rufus's back as he studied the phone. The apartment was somewhere between see-your-breath and freeze-your-balls-off; in another hour, when the radiators kicked on, it would hover right below hell's-eternal-flames and right above simmering-in-your-own-swamp-ass. Pauly Paul had either died or passed out, because their floor was quiet, and the city was a cicada song just getting started.

Five minutes later, the phone buzzed in his hand.

"Hello?"

She was already talking with that same frenetic speed. "—name's Shareed Baker. Who is this?"

"How did you get this number?"

"Is this Sam Auden?"

"Let's say it is. I'm going to ask you again: how did you get this number?"

Her breathing sounded thin. "I've got something you want."

"I doubt that. I'm hanging up now."

"Stonefish."

A horn blatted on the street.

Rufus had turned his head as Sam spoke in clipped sentences. He pushed himself up, asking, "Sam?"

Sam shook his head.

"Yeah," the woman who called herself Shareed said in his ear. "I thought that'd get you."

"What do you know about Stonefish?"

"That's going to cost you. But it's good."

"What do you—"

"A hundred thousand dollars. Bring it to—"

The laugh broke out of Sam, all glass edges and bitterness. "Who the fuck is this, really? A hundred thousand dollars. Nice."

The silence on the other end of the call had a confused quality to it. "Well, make me an offer."

"Ok, let's see, my boyfriend owes me something in the four-digit range. So, how about, zero fucking dollars and zero fucking cents. Quit wasting my fucking time."

Rufus sat up on his knees. "Don't tell people I owe you money."

"Ten thousand," Shareed said.

"Give me a break," Sam said. "You don't have anything."

"That's not what Lew Frazer thinks."

Sam realized he was clutching the sheet. He forced himself to release it. "If you've got something, and if it's as good as you say it is, I could scrape together a couple of thousand. If. I'm going to be the judge of that."

"Two thousand. In advance."

Sam grunted. He did a mental tally, his savings versus the current expense of living in a city where sometimes a hot dog cost six fucking dollars. He lowered the phone to his chest and asked Rufus, "Is the BlueMoon ok for a meet?"

Rufus was frowning. "You're not gonna bring some shitstain in there, are you? I don't want Maddie getting caught up in something."

"I don't know."

"Can I come?"

Nodding, Sam raised the phone and said, "There's a

place called the BlueMoon Diner."

This time, the silence was fractional before she blurted, "Eleven. No, ten thirty."

"Ten thirty," Sam said and disconnected.

"Who was that?" Rufus asked before Sam could even set the phone aside.

"I don't know." Sam scooted to the edge of the bed, stood, and got his jeans—folded—out of his ruck. As he stepped into them, he said, "She called herself Shareed."

Rufus climbed off the bed and nearly face-planted after getting twisted in the sheets. He threw the blankets back onto the mattress before asking, "You don't know who you're meeting, but they want money? For what, exactly?"

"Information."

Rufus grabbed his jeans from the floor—the knees had been blown out from years of wear and tear. "It's always a lot of fun trying to make sense of your vagueness."

As his head popped through the collar of the t-shirt, Sam said, "When I got out. When I left the Army, I mean. You remember what that dickhole said? All those dead soldiers?"

"I remember. We had a fight about it." Rufus pawed through a pile of laundry before yanking free a long-sleeve thermal with a hole at the collar. "So it's information about dead soldiers?"

"Maybe."

This time, Rufus looked at Sam. "Are we going to fight about it again if I ask for answers that are more than one word? I mean, 'information' was good. Three syllables, even. But some rando calling at the ass-crack of dawn, demanding money in exchange for sus intel is not how I like starting the day."

"I don't know what she has." Sam dug through the ruck

again and considered the Beretta M9. After a moment, he slid it behind the waistband at the small of his back and pulled the long t-shirt over it. Under his coat, it would be invisible. "Hurry up. I want to watch the diner until the meet."

They took a taxi. The back of the cab smelled like body odor and an animal stink like livestock; the driver was a shriveled white man with stringy hair to his shoulders, and Sam guessed he had chosen to be part of the problem rather than part of the solution. In morning traffic, it took them fifteen minutes to get to Hell's Kitchen. They stopped three blocks away from the BlueMoon, Sam paid the driver, and they got out.

The wind sliced off the Hudson, shrieking up the concrete canyons, and Sam was grateful for the heavy Patagonia jacket. Rufus, on the other hand, huddled inside his hoodie and jean jacket, looking more miserable with every passing second. Sam's watch said eight forty-five, which meant too long for Rufus to stand outside.

"Suggestions?" Sam asked.

"We park our asses inside and drink some too-strongly-brewed coffee." Rufus put a hand on his head to keep from losing his beanie in a passing gale.

"I want to see if she brings anyone with her. Or if she has anyone following her."

"On the Richter scale of paranoia, you're kinda cranked up to eleven."

"There," Sam said, nodding at a Dunkin' Donuts with a plate-glass window that offered a sight line on the BlueMoon.

He heard Rufus sigh, but he chose not to acknowledge it.

Inside, the air smelled like fryer oil, yeast, and confectioner's sugar. A handful of customers, mainly older men but a few women, stood in line. One of the men wore a CPO jacket with iron-on letters that spelled out FUCK SATAN PRAISE JESUS on the back. A woman in a plastic hair-coloring cap was frowning at the jacket, probably deciding whether or not to throw in with the Prince of Darkness. The girl behind the counter was white, pregnant, and no older than sixteen. She looked like she needed a few of the donuts herself.

"How many?" Sam asked when it was their turn.

"Three of those chocolate ones with the sprinkles," Rufus said while pointing at the donuts in the glass case. "And I should get a coffee too, for being dragged out of bed."

"How big of a coffee," Sam asked, "and how expensive?"

The answer turned out to be very and only moderately. Sam added a plain glazed for himself, as well as a small black coffee. Then they took their place at the window. The woman in the hair-coloring cap hung around too, working on a paper tray of donut holes—or munchkins, or whatever they were calling them now—and occasionally massaging her hair through the cap, as though afraid the follicles might not absorb every drop of Thoroughbred Pony or whatever the hell color she'd chosen.

Rufus had managed to shove an entire donut in his mouth on the first try, although in his defense, Sam felt the donuts were mostly air to begin with. Rufus took a sip of coffee after, then asked, "So this Shareed lady is in the Army?"

"I don't know."

"Wouldn't she be? If she's got information on something that happened when you were active duty?"

"I don't know."

Rufus rolled shut the top of his donut bag, put a hand on his hip, and asked, "What *do* you know, then? No. What do you know that you're also going to tell me? You didn't want to talk about it before, and that's fine. It's whatever. But now we're creepin' from inside a donut shop and I feel like I deserve to know why."

On the street outside, a bike courier flew past, ringing his bell and shouting at a middle-aged man pulling a shopping cart full of books into the street. The wind rapped against the glass.

"It was a training accident," Sam said, and he was surprised to hear his own voice perfectly level. "The nickname was Stonefish; someone said that was the internal name for the project, but I don't know if that's true. They were amphibious vehicles, supposed to be a significant upgrade with all the MRAP advancements we had to figure out in Iraq and Afghanistan. The next best thing from Conasauga Solutions. It stormed; the NWS issued a flash flood warning, but they either didn't know or they didn't care. Two of the vehicles capsized. Fourteen soldiers drowned." His breath fogged the glass, and then the patch of fog shrank, and then it was gone. "Someone I… cared about died. He was an NCO. A sergeant. Not when they capsized. Shit, I am telling this all wrong. They said it was his fault. He killed himself." His hands were shaking, and he steadied them against his legs. "Went— that was his name—Went wouldn't have done that. Ordered them to cross if it wasn't safe. He was always cautious. Too careful for a soldier. I thought the whole thing smelled wrong. Lew Frazer had just made captain, and he was the golden boy, his star on the rise. I asked too many questions. Nobody liked that. I left because…." Because of Went. Because of the MPs who showed up at my door. Because of the warning passed word of mouth that I was fucking myself over every time I asked another question. Because I realized it didn't matter; Went was gone.

He replayed his words. He heard his own rambling attempts to explain. Face hot, he stared through the washed-out reflection in the glass and at the street beyond.

Rufus shifted, met Sam's gaze briefly in the window, then he seemed to focus on BlueMoon across the street. His free hand found Sam's and gave it a squeeze. "How much was this Shareed lady asking for? A hundred thousand?"

A barking laugh escaped Sam. "She's new to this. Or not good at it. Or both. She had no idea how much to ask for." He hesitated and said, "She used Lew's name. She knew I'd bite."

Rufus's eyes cut across the glass once more, this time lingering on Sam's reflection. "If you left the Army years ago, what's any of this matter? In October—that guy Jonny—he said Lew had been looking for you. But why? What's it *matter*?"

The question had a jack-in-the-box answer, and Sam wasn't ready for that, so he settled for saying, "It matters to me."

The conversation stalled there. On the other side of the glass, the city thrummed with an energy that Sam felt totally cut off from. Twice he spotted women he thought might be Shareed approaching the BlueMoon, but neither woman entered the diner. Ten thirty crept past. Then eleven.

The teen mom behind the counter said they needed to order something or get out.

"Where the fuck is she?" Sam muttered as he paid for sausage-egg-and-cheese croissants.

By twelve thirty, he gave up and jerked his head at the door, and Rufus followed him out into the cold.

CHAPTER
FOUR

"Shareed's on my shit list," Rufus said, a plume of white settling in the air on an exhale. The door to Dunkin' Donuts fell shut behind him with a *clang* of jingle bells that hadn't been removed postholiday. "Give her a call. Better yet, let me. I'm going to tell her how much I appreciate losing out on a morning quickie." Rufus held his hand out expectantly.

Sam pulled up the call log, hesitated, and then passed over the phone.

Rufus tapped the most recent number and put the phone to his ear.

"Cyber 44," a woman said in an overanimated voice.

"Uh, is this Shareed?" Rufus asked.

"Shareed? No, this is Kim."

"Is Shareed there?"

"I think you have the wrong number, buddy. Shareed doesn't work here."

Rufus glanced at Sam while asking, "Hang on, what am I calling? Is this a sex hotline?"

"We're a fucking internet café, you asshole." Kim hung up.

Rufus pulled the phone away. "Shareed called from an internet café." He brought up the browser on Sam's phone, typed in the business name, then said, "Just south of us on Forty-Fourth Street."

Sam frowned. "She'd be stupid to still be there."

Rufus was scrolling through Cyber 44's website. "They have an actual café inside, with something called Buckaroo Coffee on the menu... four shots of espresso, six pumps of vanilla syrup—*God*. Maybe Shareed couldn't make it because she had a heart attack from the coffee." Rufus tucked the phone into Sam's pocket. "We can go check," he suggested. "See if she's dead in a little computer booth."

"Jesus Christ," Sam said as he nudged Rufus to start walking. "This fucking city."

Rufus led the way downtown toward West Forty-Fourth. The cross streets were heavy with early afternoon foot traffic: tourists lost in the pursuit of Times Square, delivery employees pulling carts heavy with packages, and bike messengers swerving in and out of traffic, creating chaos for everyone in their wake. Things were a bit calmer between Ninth and Tenth Avenue at least. There was the drone of ever-constant construction, sure, but Rufus and Sam also passed by quiet apartment buildings—their fire escapes heavy with pristine snow—ground floor storefronts advertising morning yoga and evening dance lessons, a wine bar that didn't open until five o'clock, as well as a bougie-looking secondhand furniture store selling fashionable accent pieces at price points that were most certainly *not* what Rufus thought of when secondhand shopping.

On the corner of Forty-Fourth and Tenth, across from a UPS drop off and nearly engulfed by overhead scaffolding, was a dark window with a neon light advertising: Cyber 44. A Pride flag, almost entirely covered in a thick layer of dust, hung lopsided underneath it.

"I don't trust this place's health grade," Rufus said. "Shareed definitely died here."

"At least she died supporting the homos." Sam yanked the door open. "After you."

"Such a gentleman," Rufus said while walking in. He pulled his sunglasses off, the café so dim he would have likely collided with a table before seeing it.

A counter, barely big enough for the register and ancient laptop beside it, was shoved into the far left corner and currently unoccupied. Deeper inside was what looked like individual desks set up with towers, monitors, and gaming chairs that once upon a time had been nice but were now reaching the ends of their lifespan. Rufus didn't see any coffee bar. Tiptoeing into the dark space, Rufus moved all the way to the end before turning and casually walking back toward the door so he was able to study the illuminated faces of café patrons.

"Excuse me?" that same excited, almost aggressive, voice said into the quiet.

Rufus stopped, looked behind him, and saw a middle-aged woman approaching. She was holding a broom and dustbin and was what they called big boned. She had short black hair and wore some t-shirt with a logo Rufus assumed was for a video game. "Just looking for a friend," he said quickly.

"You gotta pay if you come into this area—hang on.

Did you just call?"

"Just?"

"A few minutes ago?"

"Like ten or fifteen," Rufus answered.

"I am not running a sex line!" Kim shouted, startling a few patrons, but otherwise they didn't get up from their chairs. "This is an upstanding business! Get out, you skinny little shit."

Rufus backed up the remaining steps before bumping into Sam, still in the doorway. While hastily pulling Sam with him, Rufus shouted back, "It was an honest mistake!"

"And you wonder why," Sam murmured as they tumbled outside. He raised his eyebrows. "No Shareed, huh?"

Kim opened the door and continued their conversation, "Honest mistake my fat ass, boy. I have to fight tooth and nail for every fucking customer I got, and you casually toss out there my time would be better spent as a purveyor of pornography."

"Good Lord, woman," Sam said. He caught Rufus's arm. "We're going."

Rufus shoved his sunglasses back on while countering, "The porn industry brings in like, 100 billion a year, so yeah, maybe you could afford a feather duster if you switched over."

Kim dropped the dustbin and launched after Rufus with the broom.

"Holy shit, lady!" Rufus ran toward the end of the block. "Give me a break, I'm just looking for a friend," he insisted a second time. "She made a phone call from your café this morning. Sam, tell her, before she tries to break my legs!"

"I feel like I should let this play out," Sam said, leaning against the window. "It's like Animal Planet. Fuckheads of

New York. See them in their natural habitat."

"*Sam*," Rufus cried, dodging when Kim got close.

She was huffing and puffing something about feather dusters in the general vicinity of Rufus's asshole before managing to knock the broom between his legs and Rufus crashed to the frozen sidewalk. Standing over him triumphantly, Kim said, "When you see God at those pearly gates, you tell him Kim Kawabe sent you."

"Sam!"

"Christ Almighty." Sam ripped the broom from Kim's hand and pointed the handle at her. "Lady, chill the fuck out. Rufus, get your ass up. Back to your corners, or whatever you say after a fucking Manhattan meet-and-greet."

Rufus took the chance to skuttle backward like a crab.

Kim, seeming unfazed by the cold, put her hands on her big hips and gave Sam a long, lingering once-over. "Sam, huh? You're not from around here, I take it."

"The basic human decency probably gave it away."

"The phone call—" Rufus tried as he got to his feet.

"Shut up, I hate you," Kim snapped at Rufus. She said to Sam, "You can ask me about a phone call, though."

Sam's eyebrows went up again, but all he said was "A woman who called herself Shareed. It would have been early this morning. Sometime after eight."

Kim pursed her lips together like she was reluctant to speak, but went ahead with "I don't know about the name, but yeah, I had a lady pay to use the phone this morning."

"What did she look like?"

Kim narrowed her eyes as she watched Rufus join Sam's side, still rubbing his ass. "Black. Pretty. About my age. Kept her hair real short—shorter than mine. She kinda gave me the look, you know? But she didn't hang around long enough for me to offer some coffee."

"Local?"

"No way. I give ten percent discounts to the hotels around here. She had one of my coupons. Not that it mattered—it was a phone call. I charged her a quarter."

Sam threw a look at Rufus and then turned back to Kim. "What hotels? I need a list."

"Hang on. She was a little jittery, but she didn't cause any trouble. You're not trying to give her a hard time or something, are you? Are you really her friend?"

"Didn't we say that like three—"

"Red, I swear to fuck, if you open your mouth again, I'll hit you with the dustbin next. I'm talking to Tall, Dark, and Brooding."

"More like we've got business," Sam said. "She didn't show up for a meeting, and it's important. We're not going to give her any grief."

Kim was considering that. "People in Pods."

Rufus opened his mouth, then shut it.

"That's the name of the hotel," Kim explained. "It's up the block on Forty-Fifth. Shit internet service over there. Those walls are like five feet of concrete or something. I don't know. But a lot of my customers come from there because they can't get any service."

"Did she make any other calls? Do anything else? Say anything?"

"Just the three calls and then she left."

Rufus looked at Sam. "She called you twice, right?"

Sam nodded. "So who else did she call?"

"Can you star-sixty-nine that?" Rufus asked Kim next.

She ignored Rufus and addressed Sam. "I've had other calls made since eight this morning."

"God damn it," Sam said. "What about the phone company, records, that kind of thing?"

Kim puffed herself up again. "People come to Cyber 44 because they trust that their access to information will be respected and kept private. I'm not about to go digging through call records to find out who this lady phoned. It could have been her mother, for all I know. And that ain't my business." She hesitated, then said to Sam, "You know, I swing both ways."

"I don't." He shoved Rufus ahead of him. "Come on."

CHAPTER
FIVE

People in Pods apparently offered the low-price-point option for pod-based accommodations in the Five Boroughs. Sam was able to piece that together from a sun-faded flyer taped to the inside of the hotel's front door. The flyer said, *People in Pods offers the low-price-point option for pod-based accommodations in the Five Boroughs.* Right, Sam thought. Because the high-price-point option is competing with the Four Seasons.

Outside, the hotel's frontage consisted of plate-glass windows, stainless-steel trim, and brick that had been recently smeared with what Sam fervently hoped was dog shit. Inside, the lobby looked like something Andy Warhol might have slapped together on an acid trip after someone told him to "make it look like the future": aggressively bright primary colors, lots of chrome, and speckled linoleum that was probably designed to hide dirt tracked in off the street. Boy-band music thundered through the small space from speakers mounted in the corners, but if the volume—or the quality—bothered the bored twenty-somethings lounging and flipping pages, ironically perhaps, in outdated copies of *Time Out New York*, they gave no sign of it. One girl was actually asleep across an ottoman, head hanging off the edge; Sam wondered if all that blood pooling on her brain was a hazard, but he figured it couldn't be any worse than five minutes of dealing with the city outside.

"I hate BTS," Rufus said, addressing the music. "I hate that I can recognize them, actually. I need to hang out with Pauly Paul more often."

"That might actually be worse," Sam said as they approached the desk.

The clerk was youngish, bro-ish, with an expensive-looking haircut and, defying the odds, a popped collar. He was pretending to read *Atlas Shrugged*.

"I need to talk to one of your guests," Sam said.

Bro looked up, not raising his head exactly, but his eyes, which gave him a much more "snotty rich boy forced to take his first job" sort of expression. "Uh, ok. And?"

"Never mind." Sam started around the desk, heading for the elevator on the far wall.

Bro shoved the novel aside, stood from the desk, and jogged after Sam. "Hey, *man*. You can't come in here if you're not paying for a room." He moved to cut Sam off at the elevator bank, slapping his hand over the Up button.

"Man?" Sam asked.

"Are you deaf?"

Rufus hurried after the two, wrapped both hands around one of Sam's arms, and yanked him backward. "Don't whip out your dick," he whispered harshly. To Bro, he said, "Don't call him Man or Buddy or Pal or whatever Long Island bullshit you were raised with, ok? Thanks."

"I told you I want to talk to one of your guests," Sam said. "Did you not understand something?"

Rufus grabbed Sam by the chin and met his eyes. "Try offering her name."

Bro had squared his shoulders and puffed his chest out as he watched the two. He fixed his collar—made it poppier, somehow—and gave Sam an expectant "you dumb shit" kind of look.

"Shareed Baker." Sam bared his teeth. "Now."

"How about a 'please'—"

"Don't push your luck," Rufus said over Bro.

Jutting his jaw and making a scoffing sound like he'd been told to pick up his dirty socks, Bro walked back to the counter, pausing a few times to make sure they followed, and then tip-tapped at the keyboard for a moment. Sam was slow making his way back to the desk; he wanted to see the phone, which was on the clerk's side of the divider. Bro found the information, dialed an extension, and brought the receiver to his ear.

"I bet you wear cargo shorts in summer, right?" Rufus asked Bro as he sidled up to the desk. "Brown belt?"

"Dude, shut up."

"Backward baseball hat," Rufus added. "Because it makes you look *cool*."

Bro rolled his eyes and said after a few more seconds, "No one's picking up."

"She's probably taking a nap," Sam said. "I'll just go knock on her door. Which pod is she in?"

Bro put the receiver down on the cradle. "*Guy*." He said it on purpose, Sam knew. "You can't go upstairs. You're not a guest, and she's not answering the phone. If you don't leave, I'm calling the cops."

"Fine," Sam said and headed for the door.

He waited outside for Rufus to catch up.

"You know," Rufus said casually, letting the door fall shut before joining Sam on the sidewalk. "I think you could take him. You might even win."

Sam snorted. "He was wearing a Brooks Brothers polo, which means he belongs to that special group of incompetent fuckups who are protected by the Geneva Convention. How do we get back inside?"

Rufus looked like he was trying really, really hard not to laugh. "Let's try a side entrance or something. Maybe we can catch an employee taking out trash or accepting a delivery."

"Tell me if I miss it," Sam said, "in case in Manhattan a service entrance is actually a manhole or a rusty fire escape or a Slip 'N Slide that takes you straight to hell."

They headed down the block and turned at the intersection. Several plain steel fire doors studded this side of the building, and as Rufus had predicted, one of them was propped open with an overturned plastic crate. Sam slowed his pace, trying to look like this was all routine, and pulled open the door. The hallway on the other side was unremarkable—tan walls, fluorescent lights, a bulletin board with health and safety notices. It led in the general direction of the lobby and Bro-clerk. A narrow staircase, probably not up to code, climbed to Sam's right.

"Third floor," Sam said over his shoulder as he started up the steps.

Following close behind, Rufus asked, "How do you know?"

"Because he pressed Transfer and then 90308. And unless she's on the 90th floor, I'm guessing she's in 308."

"When you're sneaky, but also kinda crabby, I'll be honest, I get a chub from it."

"I know," Sam said and took the rest of the stairs two at a time.

When they exited the stairwell, they were in a section of the hotel obviously intended for guests. The high-traffic carpet was brightly patterned. LED bulbs gave a warmer, softer light than the fluorescents downstairs. The walls had some sort of pink-and-silver-flecked paper that was apparently approved by the Andy Warhol Commission-on-the-Future-and-wait-this-is-a-hotel. Plastic plaques mounted by each door indicated the number.

It wasn't like the clickbait images Sam had seen online, pictures from Tokyo or who knew where, of people climbing into coffin-sized openings stacked on top of each other. Pods—in the US, anyway—apparently meant very, very, small hotel rooms. They passed an open door; the sound of movement came from within, and Sam could see the bunkbeds and the sliding door to a bathroom with approximately the same dimensions as a matchbook. In front of the open door stood a housekeeping cart stacked with dime-sized soaps and shampoo and conditioner capsules, everything portioned so small it wouldn't have been enough to wash a cat. A key card propped against a stack of business cards that said *Your room was cleaned by* and then a line where someone had scribbled what Sam thought might say *Korby*. Toilet paper. Plastic-wrapped foam cups. Towels.

"Your washcloths are bigger than those," Sam whispered.

Rufus was too busy shoving shampoo capsules in his pocket to respond, and Sam kept going before he had to decide whether hotel theft was worth intervening in.

308 stood halfway down the hall. The door was closed and, when Sam touched the handle, locked. He considered the door for a moment, considered knocking. Then, instead, he moved back down the hallway to the open door

and the housekeeping cart. Whoever was straightening up—presumably Korby—was humming something with a fantastic amount of camp. Sam took the keycard and went back to 308.

"Unless now's not convenient," Sam said, glancing at Rufus's bulging pockets.

"Give me a break. Shampoo's expensive." Rufus held up one of the capsules. "Look at this: coconut. I'm gonna smell great for the next week."

"Mother of God," Sam said under his breath and tapped the keycard against the reader.

A green light flashed. The electronic lock disengaged. He eased the door inward, anticipating the resistance of a swing lock or chain. Nothing. Cool air washed past him, carrying the smell of vinegar, urine, and coconut. Sam listened. Nothing again.

When he stepped into the room, he let out a breath like he'd been socked in the gut. The woman on the bunk was dead. He knew in the first instant; it was one of those skills that, once you learned, you couldn't unlearn. Black, on the easy side of middle age, dressed in discount-store slacks and a plasticky-looking polka-dot blouse, she had kicked off one flat, and her stockinged foot made her look caught off guard and vulnerable.

The story, if you wanted to believe it, was all laid out: a syringe and needle; doubled-over foil and the metal cap from a glass-bottle Sprite; a blue Bic lighter; the tubing eased around her upper arm.

"Fuck me," Sam said. "You'd better call Erik."

CHAPTER
SIX

After Jake Brower had been murdered last summer, Rufus had been uncertain of his future as a confidential informant. And as concern for where his next paycheck would come from grew, he'd been transferred with no warning to the care of Detective Weaver of Major Cases. Erik had quickly proven to be Jake's opposite in every way. He was impatient, foul-mouthed, a habitual ballbuster who never let Rufus get away with even half the shit Jake had turned a blind eye to. But even though they weren't friends—would never be in the way he had been with Jake—Rufus liked Erik. He'd been solid during the fiasco regarding Rufus's mother and her killer, Jimmy Sirkosky, and Erik also put up with Sam as being part of the Rufus O'Callaghan care package.

Sort of.

Sam was a civilian, after all, so him being anywhere near a crime scene tended to rub Erik the wrong way. Rufus found that in these situations, for as long as Sam planned to be in New York—and no, Dr. Donna, he didn't want to address that particular anxiety, let's talk about some of my other upsetting and intrusive thoughts, thank you very much—keeping interactions between Sam and Erik as brief as humanly possible typically yielded the most positive results. And this one? Rufus had consolidated it to: help, there's a dead lady here and no, we didn't do anything wrong.

"Erik said he's on his way," Rufus said into the uncomfortable stillness of the room. He tucked his burner into his pocket while watching Sam hover over the dead woman. "Let's go. It smells like piss in here."

Sam didn't move.

"Sam," Rufus prompted. "Come on."

"This is our chance," he said. "Let's take a look before Erik makes us bounce."

Rufus raised both hands in a sort of dramatic what-can-you-do gesture. "Take a look at what? She OD'd. Find her wallet, check her ID, but she looks like how Cyber Kim described her. It's Shareed, I bet, and she made the life choice that mama always warned me about."

"She OD'd right before she was going to meet us to sell information? She traveled halfway across the country so she could blow me off and shoot up?" Sam frowned and squatted next to the bed, leaning closer to examine the dead woman.

Rufus crossed his arms, aware of his own agitation and defense. "I don't think she wanted to sell you anything legit, babe."

"What does that mean?"

"It means, she needed money for a habit. Case in point." Rufus nodded at the body with a jut of his chin.

"So she flew from Georgia to New York City and called me."

"Maybe she was already living here."

"But she picked me."

"Your identity isn't hidden like mine is. She could have... fuck, I don't know, read some old news article online, saw your name, found your number in the White Pages, thought you'd be an easy play."

"Because I'm an obvious mark. Gullible, disposable cash, that kind of thing." Sam straightened. "Somebody did this to her. What aren't you seeing?"

"I didn't say any of that, Sam. Don't put words in my mouth," Rufus answered, shoulders now at his ears.

"I just don't get what you're not seeing. She called me. She had information on Lew, on Stonefish. And now she's dead. That's a pretty simple a, b, c to me."

Rufus snorted before he could smother the sound. "If she'd been shot execution-style, yeah, I'd be right there with you. Blunt force trauma, sure, someone did her in. But she OD'd. Probably on some godawful shit she bought behind a fucking dumpster. There's nothing here except one sad woman who won't wake up tomorrow."

"Why me? Why Stonefish? Why not some fucking captain who's sitting on stolen equipment or covering up his buddy's sexual assault charge? When nobody else believed you that your mom's killer was active again, I believed you. I don't get why you're being so fucking stupid about this."

Rufus could feel the flush in his chest, his neck, his freckled cheeks. His underarms began to sweat. "I'm *not* stupid." He pulled out his phone again, checked the time, put it back. "We've got maybe ten minutes, if Erik isn't driving with the siren on."

Sam's posture was stiff. His words were clipped and his gaze locked on the floor as he said, "I didn't say you were stupid. I said you were being stupid." He blew out a breath, shook his head, and opened his mouth as though he might say more. Then he shut his mouth again and moved into the tiny bathroom.

Rufus waited until Sam was out of sight before he removed a pair of black winter gloves from his jacket pocket. They were cheap knockoffs of the touchscreen friendly brand and didn't actually work as advertised. They'd likely disintegrate if they got wet, but they'd been free (lifted from a street vendor in Chinatown) and maybe they'd at least keep Rufus from leaving any fingerprints. He found the woman's purse easy enough—on the floor near the head of the bunk. It was red pleather, sure, but as far as pleather went, it was nice quality, shiny, with no cracks or signs of wear. Rufus took out the wallet, flipped it open, and stared at the driver's license for Shareed Baker. Rufus looked from the shitty DMV photo, to the woman, then back at the photo.

It was Shareed all right.

Absently, Rufus thought that even in death, Shareed looked better than the government-issued ID.

Shareed had a debit card, pharmacy card, no credit cards, but in the zipper compartment, plenty of cash.

Rufus hesitated, took out the bills, counted. Just over a hundred bucks in small change. He swallowed his pride, which actually hurt a little, then called, "Sam?"

Sam's voice sounded resonant against the bathroom tile. "Huh?"

"Come here."

When Sam emerged from the bathroom, he paused, eyes fixed on the cash, and said, "Shit."

"There's more than enough here to buy street drugs." Rufus held up the wallet. "The wallet and purse are nice. Like, not something she's been dragging around for twenty years."

"So she's not hard up."

Rufus shrugged one shoulder. "If I was hard up, which I usually am, I wouldn't carry this much cash on me. I mean, I do, but I buy information, so really, do I even have money?"

After a moment, Sam grunted and returned to the bathroom.

"I'm keeping it," Rufus called. He tucked the cash into his pocket. "Fuck this day." That was more to himself.

Returning the wallet to the purse, Rufus crouched and set it back where he'd found it on the floor. He got down on his knees to check under the bed, a habit when rummaging through other people's lives. There was always good stuff under the bed. Usually porn. Vintage of course, because porn was all online nowadays, only a credit card number away. Not that Rufus paid for porn. Why pay for fantasies when he lived with the real thing?

Momentarily derailed by his own thoughts, Rufus nearly missed the small dark object just out of reach. He wriggled underneath the cramped space to grab... a phone.

Rufus said from under the bed, "I found another goodie."

This time, when Sam emerged he said, "Bathroom's a dead end unless you want Vidal Sassoon products. And I realize as I say that that you probably want to take them, so don't, because you already stole the hotel stuff. What did you find?"

Rufus got himself out from under the bed and held up the phone. "And behold, a dinosaur. A living relic of our past. The Motorola RAZR."

"Holy shit. Maybe she *was* hard up."

Rufus worked hard not to smile as he flipped the phone open. "The days of yore. Remember having to tap three times to get the letter you wanted and fuck if you missed it?" He checked the photos and text history, but nothing. Rufus opened the call logs next and his brows drew together. "She made some calls yesterday. Back-to-back-to-back. Same number."

Sam took out his phone, copied the number, and placed the call on Speaker. On the second ring, a youngish man's voice answered, "Javits Center, this is Kenneth, how may I direct your call?"

For a moment, Sam was silent, his expression calculating. "I'm sorry, I was given this number for..." He let his voice trail off. "I can't remember the actual name, I'm sorry."

Kenneth, eager to please, jumped in. "Well, let's see. We've got our signature New York Winter Show, the MoDe US Expo, Habitat for Halibut, and, let's see, the Northeast Regional Franchise Convention."

"It must be MoDe, although I have no idea what that stands for."

"More Defense for a Safer United States, I believe is the full title."

"That's it," Sam said. "The event is still running?"

A note of doubt entered Kenneth's voice. "It began today, sir. Are you sure—"

Sam disconnected the call. "She didn't just come here to talk to me. And she didn't just come here now because the timing was convenient. She called the Javits how many times? And she made a third call this morning from the cybercafé. It all ties together somehow, and it got her killed."

"You think the State killed a woman who prefers

pleather and flip phones because they believe she's trying to sell Uncle Sam's secrets?" And then Rufus's gaze cut to the hotel door as it creaked open and he said, "Oh. Hi, Erik."

CHAPTER
SEVEN

It took them two hours to shake off Weaver. Once they managed that—and it wasn't easy, because the detective hadn't been pleased to find them in the room, and he'd been even less satisfied with the story they'd been able to give him—the walk was short. Short, but miserable in the late-December wind howling through the city.

The Javits Center was an amalgamation of see-through boxes, all glass and steel supports bristling on the bank of the Hudson River. Slush gathered at the base of the walls, but the rest of the sidewalk had been shoveled and salted, the granules crunching under Sam's boots as they approached. Flags snapped restlessly, a reminder of how civic and patriotic the Javits Center was. The whole thing reminded Sam of a greenhouse taken over by Young

Republicans who were also undergrad architecture majors.

Inside, a wall of warmer air met them with the smell of wet winter gear, a cocktail of colognes, and overheated bodies. Voices echoed from the high, open spaces, rebounding off glass and cement. Every sound seemed amplified, in spite of the crush of bodies as people zipped back and forth through the concourse. Sam stepped to one side to clear the doorway, unzipped his coat, and rubbed his mouth.

"Jesus Christ. And I thought the subways were bad."

"It's definitely busier than I expected," Rufus agreed as he took off his sunglasses. "The name made me think, like, eight old guys in a musty room." He glanced at Sam. "Are you going to be ok in here? If you want to wait outside…." Rufus trailed off at the suggestion.

Sam released his breath slowly. Then he shook his head. Pointing at a banner over the escalators that announced *MoDe US Expo*, he asked, "Do we just walk in, or…."

Rufus made a humming sound while looking around the expansive room. "Oh, it looks like those ticket booths over there are open. Did you want to actually check the conference out?"

"Do you have a better idea?"

"Well. No. Not really."

"Neither do I."

Sam plunged into the maelstrom of bodies. A woman in stiletto heels, with a dog riding in the massive bag she carried, glared at Sam as she shrieked something into her phone in what sounded like an Eastern European language. An older man in a pinstriped banker's suit shouldered past Sam, raising a hand as he bellowed "Roderick" at someone across the room. A pair of middle-aged twins in matching trench coats and, underneath, sagging rainbow spandex, waved batons at Sam as though directing traffic.

When he got to the ticket booth, he was sweating.

"May I help you?" She was petite, young, her hair in tight cornrows, her eyes wrinkled with amusement.

"You can get me out of this puckering anus of a city," Sam muttered as he took out his wallet.

The girl made a noise that left no doubt as to its meaning, which could mostly be summarized as *This guy is an asshole and every assumption I made about him has just been proven right.*

Sam chose to ignore the communication. "Two for the MoDe Expo."

"That will be five hundred and forty-five dollars."

"Is that some kind of joke? Two hundred and seventy something dollars for a fucking convention?"

"No, sir. That's five hundred and forty-five dollars each. There's also an add-on option for two dinners and a meet-and-greet luncheon, plus the early morning and midmorning kaffeeklatsches and—"

"Is there a sale? A discount? What about veterans?"

Rufus, having kept up well enough when Sam had barreled his way through the crowds, was now doubled over at Sam's side, hands on his knees. "I can't pay that. It's giving me the shakes."

"Active-duty—" the girl began, arching her elaborately done eyebrows.

"Never mind," Sam said. "For fuck's sake, this fucking city." He didn't have that much cash, which meant using a bank card, which he liked even less than paying full price for this fucking debacle whose sole purpose, he imagined, was for old white men to give each other handjobs. That was only partially figurative, he decided. But since Shareed Baker had tracked him down, he figured he wasn't giving too much away by using the card now. He paid. He scribbled his name on the receipt hard enough to tear the thermal paper. And then he took the badges that the girl slid under the partition and passed one to Rufus.

A guard—if you could call a middle-aged woman in an ill-fitting blazer and a Mary Tyler Moore wig a guard—checked their badges and waved them onto the escalator. They rode down to the exhibition hall in silence. Relative silence, anyway.

"Any ideas on how to figure out who Shareed wanted to track down?" Sam asked as the hub of voices faded above them and the softer babble from the hall below swelled.

Rufus absently worried the plastic edge of his badge with a fingernail. "Maybe we should find a schedule. They list exhibitors on that, I bet." He glanced up at Sam before adding, "Maybe someone's here from Benning?"

After a moment, Sam jerked his head in a nod. "Do they have a program with a list of people? Or do we just wander around?"

"Hang here for a second." Rufus patted Sam's arm as they stepped off the escalator. He slipped into the sea of people, heading toward a small booth off to the left with a banner overhead reading: WELCOME.

Rufus talked to a very blonde and very perky woman, took a handful of printouts she politely forced into his hands, and made his way back to Sam. He sifted through the pile, leaned to one side of the escalator wall to dump what he apparently deemed to be junk into a trashcan, and ended up with a fully colored program listing events, speakers, locations, and times.

He gave it to Sam. "I don't speak government. You look at that."

The exhibition hall was overwhelming in its own way. The roar of voices. The maze of booths and dividers. The underlying rush of ventilation fans like someone breathing heavily in the distance. But what caught and kept Sam's attention were the people. Unlike the exhibition hall above, the demographic here skewed heavily male and predominantly white, with the 50+ bracket abundantly represented. They wore expensive suits and shook hands and talked too loudly, some of them the kind that had to drop numbers—the cost of their car, the cost of their pool, the cost of their wife—while others had the predatory, dead-eyed look of men for whom numbers were less important than power. The women Sam did see seemed to fit one of two types: either the kind who were clearly ex-military and who carried themselves with the kind of invisible armor that Sam was all too familiar with, having worn it himself while he was still serving; or the kind who were purebred corporate, fake hair and fake teeth and fake tits, and who had the brassy self-assurance that came from trying too hard to be one of the boys. Sam was sure he was being unfair; someone in the room had to be a decent, normal person. They were probably wearing a Javits uniform.

Sam flipped through the program. Many of the events—most of them—were exclusively about and by corporations—everybody who fell under the umbrella term for this section of the population, *industry*. These were the guys who wanted to sell more guns or more tanks or more nuclear warheads—who the hell knew anymore. Two events caught his eye, though. *Summit on Wireless Communications: Key Battlefield Considerations, A Tactical Reevaluation* was sponsored by AboutFace Innovations and Red Ice, Inc., two corporate drones listed in conversation with LTC Campbell Credille, US Army. Another was *Mobile Deployables in the 21st Century: Engagement and Elimination*, hosted by Deepriver Properties and AdvaGrowth Advancements and featuring a panel headed by Major Annelise Sherman, US Army.

Sam showed the two entries to Rufus. "One is about to end," he said, "and the other starts in fifteen minutes."

"They sound riveting."

"Credille was at Benning for a time," Sam said. "I don't know Sherman, but I'd like to check them both out."

They headed through the hall, using the tiny map of the Javits Center on the program in the kind of orienteering field exercise that would have given sadistic NCOs the world over a wet dream. By the time they reached the room where the first panel was being held, sweat soaked Sam's tee, bunching it under his arms, and he could feel his heartbeat in his throat. He ratcheted the emotions down as they slipped into the back of the room, and he forced himself to focus.

A skinny white guy in a skinny tie was trying to swallow the microphone.

"—real-time communication vis-à-vis operability and adverse logistical networks—"

Rufus leaned against the wall beside Sam, arms crossed, a scowl on his face. "What the literal fuck," he whispered, "is he saying? Why can't Government Yes Men just talk like regular humans?" A handful of seconds passed before Rufus added in as much snark as a whisper could have, "*Vis-à-vis*."

The moderator kept trying to break in to end the discussion, but the skinny guy was too busy deepthroating the mic to notice. Sam used the time to study the people on the stage. He had a hard time believing Shareed Baker would have tried to contact anyone on that stage—all of them, to borrow Rufus's phrase, Government Yes Men—except Credille. The lieutenant colonel was something of a fixture at Benning; he made a big deal out of his Puerto Rican ancestry, and he'd played himself up as an ordinary guy. His tightly cut dark hair was graying, and he had the hard look of a man who has grown old on the inside.

Eventually, the moderator managed to put the audience out of its misery, and Sam pressed himself to the wall as people hurried to escape. Credille was swept up by two corporate bros, men who had to be twenty years younger and with the soft, baby-faced look of men who spent exorbitant amounts on moisturizers.

"I guess we try the next one," Sam said, unable to keep the frustration from his voice. "I don't even know what I'm looking for."

The next panel was in an identical room, with an identical crowd of men who kept themselves busy on their phones and tablets, hardly bothering to pretend to be interested in the conversation on the stage. As before, the speakers were a motley of pale-faced industry types, although Sam was surprised to see two women on stage in addition to Annelise Sherman. The major was a solidly built woman, although some of that had to be the uniform, which, in true Army fashion, had probably never been flattering on anyone because it had been designed to fit everyone. Sexy pics of guys in uniform were all well and good until you actually saw an enlisted dumbass in real life in baggy trousers. Then Sam remembered certain barracks episodes and grudgingly reconsidered.

One of the women was talking too quickly into the microphone.

"—neutralize enemy combatants with an increased 0.4 percent success rate, calculated using the Stromberg factor—"

After fifteen minutes of that, Sam jerked his head at the door, and they made their way out. "This is stupid," Sam said. "And a fucking waste of a thousand dollars. Shareed called here, but we're never going to figure out who she wanted to reach or why. What am I supposed to do? Walk up to Sherman and say, 'Excuse me, Major, but I think a murdered woman was trying to reach you, but if she was, it was probably about something illegal, and you're definitely not going to want to admit you know what I'm talking about.'" He rubbed his leg—the stab wound had healed well, but the gunshot still ached, and right then, it was starting to throb. "Fuck this shit."

Rufus had waited until the pissing and cussing was out of Sam's system, and then he grabbed a fistful of his shirt and said, "Come here." He dragged Sam down a hall of closed doors. It grew less crowded and quieter the farther they went, until most of the noise was made up of muffled voices echoing from the panels within the closed rooms. Rufus came to a stop at the end, pushed Sam against the wall, and kept a hand pressed to his chest. "Stand here a minute and relax, ok? Give me this." He took the partially rolled and wrinkled program. "Just stand here." Rufus thumbed through the booklet, pausing about halfway through. He asked, "What did you call that company—Conasauga?"

"The one with Stonefish? Conasauga Solutions."

Rufus was nodding as he turned the program around and tapped a short paragraph. "They're here. See?"

"Of course they're here; they're a major defense contractor—" Sam cut himself off. "Shit. She said the information was about Stonefish."

Rufus flipped the program, studied the details, then looked over his shoulder at the way they'd come. "Their panel is going on right now. I think it's down that way. Opposite end—isn't it always?" He offered Sam a small smile. "Wanna poke your head in? Unless you'd rather go listen to that lady talk about neutralizing some more…."

"Jesus God, no," Sam muttered as he set off down the hall.

Rufus had been right; the Conasauga event was at the opposite end of the hall. The crowd had thinned somewhat after the latest set of panels had begun, which meant that Sam could move more easily down the hallway, but there were still enough people to make him wish for the good old days, when you could carry a buggy whip to make people get the hell out of your way. The faces of so many nominally straight, quasi-military white guys were starting to blur together. One industry bro in a too-modern suit—the damn thing fit him like a sausage casing—checked Sam with his shoulder, and when Sam met his glare with one of his own, he could have sworn, for an instant, he knew the guy.

Then he reached the doors for the Conasauga panel and stepped inside.

His eyes fell on Lew Frazer. He sat at the front of the room, and for a moment, Sam couldn't move, and Rufus crashed into him. The movement propelled Sam into the room, and he recovered himself enough to shuffle into the back row of seats. His eyes were still locked on Lew.

He hadn't changed much. Average height, solidly built—Lew had always liked the gym. Crew cut, but he did something to it that made him look pretty as well as regulation. He was one of those guys who, even with a deep tan from the field, looked smooth-skinned and glowing. Went had told Sam, once, drunk, that he thought Lew had a gorgeous mouth, but Sam didn't see it.

Right then, Lew was talking to an older man in a conservative blue suit, the two of them in a whispered conversation that, under closer scrutiny, looked fraught with emotion. On stage, an older white man in an even more expensive-looking suit was strutting around with the microphone, while a woman stood opposite, trying to look patient, maybe even enthusiastic, and doing a poor job of it.

"So I told Evangeline they might not like it, and they might not want it, but we're going to do it because it's the right thing to do. And Evangeline and I told those senators what we were going to do, and you should've seen them—the lot of them nervous as cats in a room full of rocking chairs!"

The audience burst into laughter that seemed, to Sam's distant awareness of it, only partially cued. Evangeline, apparently the woman on stage, offered a mile-wide smile and said in a fake aside, "That's how Del Jolly does business, everyone. Are you surprised?" And another laugh rolled through the crowd.

All of it might have been happening on another planet as far as Sam was concerned. Lew's conversation with the older man had clearly escalated, and Lew had shifted to the edge of his seat, gesticulating sharply, although he held his hands low as though trying to keep them hidden. Then Lew shot to his feet, head bowed as he snapped off something else in a low voice.

Sam pushed Rufus toward the door.

"What the—*Sam*," Rufus hissed, stumbling over his own feet. "What the hell?"

"Go," Sam muttered, shoving him again. "We've got to get out of here."

Rufus slapped both hands down on the push bar. He'd just stepped into the hallway before he was shoved sideways so hard that he crashed into a nearby table display.

Sam turned around as Industry Bro, the one who had bumped him in the hall minutes before, threw a punch at his head.

CHAPTER
EIGHT

Rufus clipped the table with his hip hard enough that there was a moment—a second, really—as he was falling to the floor, that he wondered if he'd broken the bone. He had no idea how much force it took to break a hip. Not as much as breaking a femur, that he knew. He'd read all about bone breaks after his bully at PS14 had chucked him down a flight of stairs and Rufus had broken his arm on the asbestos-ridden linoleum.

4,000 newtons of force.

And maybe he remembered that so well because he'd been a dumb kid and thought the book meant newtons as in Fig Newtons. So he'd asked the school's librarian about it, and they'd gently corrected him, which was how Rufus had come to learn that 4,000 newtons of force actually meant about 900 pounds.

Anyway. He didn't break his hip.

"*Sonofabitch*!" Rufus shouted as he hit the floor. White-hot pain, like the senses in his body momentarily lost all reason, shot up and down his hip, his leg, all the way to his toes. But when Rufus looked up from where he'd landed, all pain ceased—like his body suddenly waved a white flag and his brain had accepted its surrender. He watched a well-built guy sucker punch Sam and knock him back against the wall beside the doors they'd just exited.

"—shouldn't have shown your face again, Auden," the guy in a too-tight suit was saying as he grabbed the front of Sam's shirt, pinning him in place.

Stumbling to his feet, Rufus ran at the guy and punched him in the right kidney as hard as he fucking could. When the stranger reared back and screamed, Sam shoved him away, but the movement didn't have much force behind it—Sam still looked a little cross-eyed.

Rufus pushed the asshat out of the way, grabbed Sam's hand, and dragged him along the hall that opened back up on the lower floor's exhibition area. Over his shoulder, Rufus shouted, "Piss blood and get fucked!" He plowed through the crowd, making a beeline for the escalators, his vision tunneling, noise turning into something staticky—like an old television set with bunny ear antennas.

Rufus wasn't even entirely sure why he was running.

Instinct.

He'd survived this long because he wasn't stupid enough to stick around. But being here—surrounded by rich people, powerful people, smart people talking in another fucking language—and then someone touching Sam, hurting Sam, calling Sam *by name*... Rufus knew nothing started here would end in their favor.

He didn't stop moving, didn't stop dragging Sam along, not until they were upstairs and out the glass doors of the Javits. Only then, with the salted sidewalk crunching under his every step, did Rufus stop to take a breath.

"Come on," Rufus said once he had enough air in his lungs.

He started toward Thirty-Fourth Street, looking over his shoulder a few times, but no one was following them. It was just Rufus, Sam, the *clank* of the flagpole overhead, and a few dozen other attendees leaving for the day, wandering in different directions to various hotels surrounding the Javits.

"Who was that guy?" Rufus finally asked. "I hope he wasn't someone important, because I punched him pretty good."

Sam rubbed his jaw. "That sucker-punching, shit-eating, pusillanimous walking cock hole is Brady Ellsworth. He looks like shit; that's why I didn't recognize him at first."

They crossed the street and Rufus tried for something lighthearted—to cut the tension. "You're cute when you talk like that."

"He's Lew's best friend—that's how he'd describe it. Lew, being an even bigger and more gaping bloody gash than Ellsworth, doesn't really have friends, though, so Brady is really more like Lew's pet troll he sends out to fuck things up."

Across from them was Fifty-Five Hudson Yards, a new skyscraper with weirdly rounded glass walls that sort of looked like LEGO pieces. Rufus didn't like it. He thought Sam probably didn't either. That is, if Sam were in the right mindset in which to take in the surrounding architecture. After passing the glass abomination of fifty-something stories, Rufus turned onto Thirty-Third to escape a wind tunnel.

On the corner, he stopped to look up at Sam. "Why would Brady appear out of nowhere just to pop you one?

Are you ok, by the way?" Rufus touched Sam's face.

"Fine. And Brady is here because Lew is here." For a moment, the tension seemed to go out of Sam, and he rested against Rufus's touch. His eyelids lowered, a heartbeat passed, and then they snapped open again, and Sam straightened. "He was in that room. The Conasauga panel, I mean. That's who I saw, and that's why I freaked the fuck out and sent us right back into Brady's path."

Rufus lowered his hand, tucked it into his jacket pocket. "Lew was in there? Which guy was he? The one talking?"

"No. Lew was sitting in the front. He was having some kind of argument—that's what it looked like, anyway."

"So… if this Brady Bunch Bitch was waiting for you, does that mean Lew saw you?"

"I don't know." Sam pinched the bridge of his nose, and his eyes shuttered for another heart-stopping moment. "No. I don't think so."

"Ok." Rufus hunched his shoulders a little before nodding to himself. "Ok," he repeated. "What do you want to do?"

A taxi was slowing down on the street as it approached them, and Sam fixed it with more than his usual level of hatred. He caught Rufus's arm and pulled him into a walk. The taxi rolled behind them, and Sam threw another look over his shoulder before walking faster.

"Fuck me," he muttered. In a louder voice, he said, "It doesn't seem like a coincidence that Shareed contacts me out of the blue, offering to sell me information about Stonefish, information that she says Lew Frazer was interested in, and then Shareed ends up dead after calling a convention where Lew just happens to be offering corporate blowjobs to the same dumbfuck company that was behind Stonefish in the first place."

"I admit," Rufus ventured after a pause. "The

probabilities of it all being chance seem slim."

"So, the next step is to fill in the blanks. What did Shareed have? Why did Lew kill her? And how?"

"Well, if she had something tangible, it wasn't left behind in that hotel room. Give me your hand."

Sam held out his hand.

Rufus took it, sliding his cold fingers between Sam's own warm ones. He thought about Edmund Burn, PhD, the third edition of *What to Do When Anxiety Strikes*. You were supposed to utilize the five senses to regain control of your body and mind, but Sam was intent on moving, was probably too agitated to stop and humor Rufus's request that he see, touch, hear, smell, and taste. So Rufus improvised and hoped that his touch would be as comforting as Sam's was when he was working himself up. "I wanted to hold your hand," Rufus lied while shrugging. "But someone back there probably would've strung me up to the flagpole by my wiener."

"Do you want to tell Erik about Lew and what we think might be going on?"

"If you *want* me to involve Erik, I will. You might have to rub burn ointment on my ass, though, because he's going to be feisty."

"Erik wouldn't be able to do anything," Sam said, more to himself than to Rufus. "I don't even know if he'd believe me. Not without something concrete."

"Then I guess we should ask more questions about Shareed," Rufus concluded. "Like, for one, why do you think Lew murdered her? I mean, *Lew* specifically. Because setting up an elaborate display meant to look like an OD…. I don't know the guy, but that seems sort of overdramatic, you know?"

"It seems like a good way to keep anyone from thinking she was murdered."

"But that wasn't my only question, Sam." Rufus looked at him. "Why do you think Lew is a murderer?"

"Because she said his name, Rufus. She said he wanted the information she had. This is Benning all over again, do you get that? Went killed himself because they pinned it on him, and nobody would look twice at Lew Frazer because they thought he'd hung the moon, even though I knew he was hiding something. Now he killed this woman, and I can't even get you to believe me. Why the fuck would I expect Erik to?"

Rufus pulled Sam to a stop. "Don't make it sound like that. I'm asking because—because I don't know who any of these people are. I don't know what happened firsthand at Benning. I barely fucking understood those stupid keywords the panelists were flinging at the audience. Shareed said Lew's name, ok I get that. Said he wanted information on Stonefish, as well. Fine. But she said your name too, and you want information too, and you surely didn't fucking kill her." Rufus worked his jaw for a minute before swallowing the softball lodged in his throat. "I don't want you having tunnel vision."

"Right." His voice was tight. "Thanks."

"Sam," Rufus protested. "I'm on your side. I'm *always* on your side."

"No, you're right. I'm obsessing. But I don't think I'm wrong about Shareed. Someone killed her."

"Then we need to prove it without a forensics or medical degree," Rufus said, offering a hesitant smile.

"Fuck, we don't even know who she is, not really."

"We can start there, then."

"Fine," Sam said as he started walking again.

CHAPTER
NINE

They walked back to Forty-Fourth and Tenth, the wind slapping Sam in the face hard enough to bring tears to his eyes. The ache in his leg had gotten steadily worse once the adrenaline from the fight with Brady had worn off, but he barely felt it now as the cold dug into him. The day's long shadows had thickened almost into night; the sun had dropped completely out of sight, and streetlights were popping on.

Cyber 44 didn't look much better in the gloom. The neon sign shed a pink glow under the scaffolding, barely enough to make out the drooping Pride flag. A hobbitish man scurried out of the cybercafé, the shopkeeper's bell jingling as the door swung shut on its closer. Sam kept his pace steady and hoped that Rufus hadn't figured out yet where they were going.

"Oh, come the fuck on," Rufus groaned as if on cue. "She almost beat me black-and-blue this morning. Let's go somewhere else."

Sam ignored him and, just to be safe, walked faster.

Inside, Cyber 44 smelled like Fuego Takis, farts, and old vinyl. The air was warm and stuffy. Kim sat behind a desk near the door. The computer monitor was angled so that Sam couldn't see it, but judging by the number of full-sized Pokémon plushies posed against the blacked-out window behind her, he thought he had a pretty good guess of what she might be doing.

"I need to use a computer," Sam said.

Kim glared at him. She was stitching up something that looked like a plush green radish, and the needle's movement quickened into hard jabs. "He's not allowed in here. He thinks this is a sex dungeon."

"I do not," Rufus interjected. "I said it was a phone sex hotline."

"Twenty minutes," Sam said, opening his wallet. He hesitated.

"Ten dollars," Kim said. "For an hour."

"I don't need an hour."

The plushie got a needle right through what was either an eye or an egg sac. "By the hour only." She yanked the needle the rest of the way through and added, "Or you can buy forty hours for three-fifty."

"I want twenty minutes," Sam said. "Why the fuck would I buy forty hours?"

"It's a better deal," Kim said with a shrug.

He paid the ten dollars, and Kim waved them down to a machine at the end of the room. It was hotter down here, all the electronics putting off heat, the fans whirring to create an ocean of white noise. At this end of the room, only one other computer was occupied. The gamer smelled like unwashed hair and medicated powder, even at a distance, and he was playing something called REVERSE GAY HAREM - MAKE THEM DO WHAT YOU WANT. It looked like this guy was mostly picking out underwear for cartoon men with incredibly unrealistic body types—

"Can we have a different one?" Sam shouted to Kim.

Whatever she shouted back, it was definitely a no, although it wasn't exactly words.

Sam pulled a seat over for Rufus, sat in another chair himself, and opened a browser. He typed in Shareed Baker.

DuckDuckGo returned a lot of results on Shareef Baker, which wasn't exactly helpful. It also offered a fair amount of suggestions about *shared bakers*, which was apparently another millennial brain-fuck trend, and Shareed Bakkar, who operated a jet ski rental in Palm Beach.

"Great," Sam muttered. "I knew this was going to be easy."

"Try some kind of military keyword with her name," Rufus suggested as he shrugged out of his jean jacket and unzipped his hoodie. "Army or Benning or something."

Shareed Baker Army yielded even more confusing results, and nothing that seemed helpful. *Shareed Baker Benning* popped up with a white-page listing that suggested that someone named Shareed Baker had, indeed, lived in Columbus, Georgia, in 2017. But that was the closest they'd gotten, so Sam tried *Shareed Baker Stonefish*, which pointed him toward an exotic-fish-and-aquarium-supply store in Queens, and *Shareed Baker Conasauga*, which populated his results with information about bakeries in the Lake Conasauga area.

"They pay those pencil-necks millions of dollars for this fucking algorithm."

"I'd love a muffin right about now," Rufus said, sort of to himself, but also sort of not. "My blood sugar's low. I think yours is too. It's too bad about the health code rating here, huh? Oh, see if Shareed has a Facebook profile."

"I thought nobody over the age of six had Facebook anymore," Sam growled, but he opened a tab and typed in the address. He had an account—barely used—but when he searched for Shareed Baker, he got only two results: one was a grandmother in Minnetonka, and the other was encouraging Sam to SEE MY LIVE VIDEO AND ALL MY PICS - CLICK HERE - I'VE BEEN SO NAUGHTY!

Rufus put a hand on the back of Sam's neck. He kneaded a little before leaning in close to whisper, "I'd like to take this moment to point out that your judgment loses some of its intensity when you, a man older than myself, are logged into an active Facebook account. But also, I'm going to remind you, in graphic detail, that I'm not six-years-old, by talking about my flaming red pubes."

"I know," Sam said, but he leaned into Rufus's touch. "I'm still picking them out of my teeth. Now stop interrupting me."

After a moment of staring at Shareed Baker's profile—the naughty one—Sam closed the tab and opened a new one. He pulled up Garrison.

Hand still on Sam's neck, Rufus stopped digging into the muscles, asking, "What's this?"

"Military version of Facebook. Fewer thongs. More guns." He signed in, ignored the demand that he pay twenty dollars a month to upgrade to a DELTA account, and typed in Shareed Baker.

Her profile was the first hit: Shareed Baker, Fort Benning CID Battalion, Criminal Investigations Special Agent (31D). The profile picture matched the woman they had found dead in the pod. When he clicked on the profile, he got a page that had been locked down. "Request Ally?" a box asked him. He clicked it, although he knew Shareed Baker would never respond, and then sat back with a sigh.

"I don't know what CID means, but she was involved in military investigations." Rufus lowered his hand as he looked at Sam. "That's like—pretty hardcore, right?"

"She investigated soldiers on their own turf, and she was a black woman doing it. Hardcore sounds about right."

Rufus checked on the Harem Gamer before scooting his chair closer to Sam's. He asked quietly, "Did you ever have any contact with her—or whatever CID is, I guess—when you were in the Army? At Benning?"

Sam shook his head. Then he took out his phone and weighed it in one hand. "But somebody has to know something about her. Hold on." He considered his options, the limited number of names in his contacts, the bridges he hadn't burned even after Stonefish. He picked what he thought his best option was and raised the phone.

"Hey." Rufus put a hand over the phone and met Sam's eyes. "I just need you to know—we—*you* don't have to do this. Not if you don't want to. We can walk out of here right now, go home, and forget today ever happened. No matter what favors or strings I've got to pull to make sure no one finds you, I'll do it."

It was harder than it should have been to say, "Thank you." Then Sam shook his head and placed the call on Speaker.

Colly picked up on the third ring. "Should I be flattered or worried?"

The guy building his REVERSE GAY HAREM—whatever the fuck that was—made an irritated noise. Sam glared at him, but he lowered the volume so that he and Rufus had to lower their heads over the phone.

"What's that supposed to mean?" Sam asked.

"You don't write, you don't call…." When the silence dragged, Colly said, "Ah. Same old Auden charm, I see."

Rufus met Sam's gaze, held up his hands, and made air

quotes while mouthing "Auden charm."

"I need a favor."

"There it is." She sighed. "What?"

"Do you know Shareed Baker? She's CID, a special agent in the Benning battalion. Was."

Colly's voice sharpened with interest. "She's dead?"

"As of this morning. You know her?"

"No, but dead CID doesn't sound good."

Sam laid out the day's events as best he could without involving Colly too much. When he'd finished, he said, "Whatever you can find out about Shareed—"

"Give me five minutes. No, hold on, the bastard might have already gone home, and I'll have to call him on his cell. Give me ten."

She disconnected before Sam could respond.

"Who was that?" Rufus whispered. "Your Army wife?"

The grin surprised Sam. "Something like that. She's an analyst; we worked together. Smarter than any of the dumbshits in command."

The gamer with the unwashed hair turned in his seat and made another irritated noise, this time leveling up his stare to death ray.

"What the fuck are you going to do about it?" Sam asked. "Motherfucker, I just saw you spend five dollars for a digital pasty collection for your gay reverse harem."

Apparently reverse gay harem time was over because the gamer scuttled to the door, the bell ringing behind him as the door wobbled shut.

"You're running off my paying customers," Kim shrieked.

"If she comes after *you* with that broom, I'm not helping," Rufus told Sam. "You said it was like Animal Planet."

Sam rubbed his forehead. "Ten fucking minutes of this."

"I can go buy some rainbow pasties for my nips and entertain you."

"Do that."

The ten minutes dragged past, and then the phone vibrated in Sam's hand. He answered on Speaker.

"She's in hot water. Was, I guess." Colly's voice was troubled. "You're sure she's dead?"

"Pretty sure."

"Well, she's AWOL. Nobody knows where she is. Are you still in New York?"

"Should I answer that?"

"Probably not. My guy in CID said she'd bailed twice on her annual drug test, and rumors had already been floating around that she was using. She was erratic. Not doing her work. Pulling old cases from storage. I think they were hoping she'd fail the drug test and they could get rid of her."

"Old cases? What old cases?"

Surprise laced Colly's voice. "I don't know. Do you want me to find out?"

"No. Thanks, Colly."

"Save the thanks. Maybe sometime just call me when you don't need something. How about that?"

Sam grunted. He reached for the End button. Then he stopped. "Did you know Lew Frazer is in New York City?"

"I knew you were still there. Are you with that guy? The cute one?"

Rufus choked and started coughing.

"Colly: Lew Frazer."

Rufus smacked Sam's bicep and whispered loudly, "Let her talk about me."

Sam glared at him and turned up the volume slightly.

"Look, I'm not saying you're wrong about what happened." Colly's voice was weary. "Yeah, that piece of shit probably made the call on Stonefish, and yeah, Went is the one who took it in the neck, and yeah, it still tears me up what Went did to himself. But you already threw away your career over this jerk. You're in a better place now, right? Don't let him get inside your head again."

"You can find out where he's staying." The thought hadn't occurred to Sam until now, but it hit him at sixty miles an hour. "He's here in some sort of official capacity; he was in uniform. So you can find out where he's staying."

"I can't—"

"Yeah, you can. You call the travel office, and you tell them you've got something you need to overnight him. You just need the hotel where he's staying, the address and room number, that kind of thing."

"Sam."

"If they ask, tell them it's classified, which they'll buy because you're intel—"

"Sam, the answer is no."

"This isn't—"

"Let it go, the thing with Lew. He's as crazy about you as you are about him. I'm not putting the two of you on a collision course."

"That son of a bitch murdered—"

"Call me sometime, Sam. Hell, call me even if it's only for another favor, the Auden way. But not about this."

She disconnected.

Sam stared at the phone. "What the ever-loving fuck?"

CHAPTER
TEN

On their way back to Rufus's tenement on East Fourth Street, Rufus had segued to grab some dinner from a Chinese restaurant called Super Flavor Plus 2. (He was uncertain of the fate of Super Flavor Plus 1.) It was a hole-in-the-wall in nearly every sense: no tables, no chairs, just the faded, backlit display of meal options hanging overhead the bulky cash register. And if you weren't a neighborhood local, you'd have no reason to know that they'd been out of shrimp chow mein since at least 2003 but had never stopped advertising it. Once his takeout containers had been loaded to the brim with hot and aromatic food, Rufus passed the auntie working the register several wrinkled bills, grabbed the knotted plastic bag, and disappeared back into the cold night.

Upon entering 4D, and after kicking off his salt-crusted Cons and dropping his jackets and hat into their usual pile on the floor, Rufus removed containers from the bag and set them all out on the floor beside the bed. He said to Sam, "I got dumplings, hot and spicy beef, and chicken lo mein." He sat on his knees before the food. "Pick your poison."

"Dumplings," Sam said, opening the closest container. Luck was on his side, apparently, and he sat back and grabbed the paper-wrapped chopsticks.

Rufus yanked open the container nearly bursting with noodles. Condensation splattered his t-shirt and he wiped it absently while saying, "So Shareed was using."

"They thought she might be using. Which is the kind of rumor someone would spread if they didn't like what she was looking into."

"Ok," Rufus answered, his tone as if he were trying to calm a wild animal. "I'll shelve that. Can I ask you something else?"

Sam made a noise around a mouthful of dumpling.

"Who did Lew murder? You said on the phone, 'that son of a bitch murdered' and then you stopped."

Sam swallowed. His voice had a flat obstinacy as he said, "Shareed."

"That's who you meant?"

"Well, he's responsible for those soldiers with Stonefish. And Went; if Lew had manned up, if he'd kept them from piling everything on a kid who was barely old enough to shave, Went wouldn't have done what he did. But I was talking about Shareed."

"If you say Lew's a piece of shit, I believe you, I swear. But we don't *know* he killed Shareed. If it wasn't an OD—don't get mad, I'm just saying—if it wasn't an OD, if she was murdered, and everything was set up to reflect this rumor that she was having drug issues…. Your Army wife made it sound like several people knew of her erratic behavior. All I'm saying is, when it comes to what happened in her hotel room, we've no idea if Lew was there."

"That's what we're trying to prove."

"It sort of sounds like we're trying to make the pieces fit Lew Frazer."

"Fine, Rufus." He set the unfinished container of dumplings aside. "What am I missing?"

"I don't know." Rufus pushed aside his own untouched food and knee-walked across the floor toward Sam. "But maybe the narrative should be: I think Shareed was murdered by someone, and not, Shareed was murdered by Lew. At least, not yet."

"Fine."

"You're just saying 'fine' because you're mad at me."

"I'm saying it because I don't know what you want me to say. You think I'm wrong. Fine. I can't prove it yet. Fine. There's not a lot left to talk about."

"I can call Erik—see if he's willing to mention anything CSU might've found."

As an answer, Sam grabbed the container and speared a dumpling.

Rufus nodded, muttered "Fine" under his breath, and got to his feet. He tugged his burner free from his pocket and dialed Erik's number. "Hello, gorgeous."

"What? Make it fast; I'm still dealing with the wreckage of a crime scene you and your butt buddy left me."

"Did you find anything interesting at the pod?"

"Sure. I found my incompetent CI and his dong bait walking all over my fucking scene. You're fishing, asshole, and I'm hanging up."

"Don't do that. Come on, I'm sorry I walked all over your scene. In my defense, there was a dead lady inside. Not that I knew she was dead. What if she'd been alive and I left her? Then you'd have a CI wanted for like, involuntary manslaughter or something."

Erik made a noise of disgust. But he didn't disconnect.

"I got you those pics of Chad yesterday, didn't I? All I'm asking for now and then is a little pat on the head. Come on, I was severely neglected as a child."

"You've got your boy toy. He can pat you on your head or your ass or wherever."

"There's something about it coming from a man with a badge."

"Don't you have someone else to bother?"

"Not really," Rufus answered. "I live and die for you."

This time, all Rufus got was a grunt. After a moment, though, Erik asked, "Have you heard about anything over at the Javits?"

Rufus's eyebrows rose and he looked toward Sam. "Maybe. Can you give me a clue?"

"There's no clue, doofus. You're my CI. I'm asking you if you've heard people talking about something at the Javits. That's the extent of it." He paused. "What about the last name Ridgeway? And if you make one of your fucking quips—"

"No quips, daddy, I promise. Should I know the name? Do you want me to?"

"That woman, Shareed, she called her from the hotel," Erik said. "See what you can find out."

"I've worked with less." Rufus hung up, sat on the floor again, and crossed his legs under him. "Erik asked if I'd heard anything happening at the Javits. Asked if I recognized the name, Ridgeway?"

"I feel like I've heard that name." Sam shrugged. "I

can't place it. If it comes to me, I'll let you know."

Rufus watched Sam stab another dumpling with his chopsticks before he busied himself balancing his noodle container on one knee, phone on the other, and did an internet search while eating. The name Ridgeway brought up a handful of the typical results Rufus expected from such a vague search. Some movie star named Bianca Ridgeway was in hot water over a nip-slip. Census records for a Manny Ridgeway who passed away last Tuesday out in the Rockaways—RIP Manny. A Zillow listing for a house on Ridgeway Street in Michigan. But at the bottom of the first Google page was a link to Conasauga Solutions, the gibberish of keywords underneath the website cutting off midsentence, but the name Evangeline Ridgeway had appeared in bold font.

Rufus clicked and was directed to a very simplistic page with a white and blue aesthetic overlaid with a sans-serif font proclaiming some very expressive talking points. Innovative! Solutions! Spirit! Restructure! He clicked around a moment before finding an option in the dropdown menu for: PROFESSIONALS. He chose that and was directed to a listing of thumbnail images showing off very white-collar folks smiling big for their employee photo. Beside each were bullet points of their education, work history, and accomplishments. Rufus scrolled down to R and found Ridgeway, Evangeline.

"Hey." Rufus turned his phone around and held it out. "Do you recognize her?"

Sam frowned. "She was on the stage. At the panel, the Conasauga one. The corporate douche was doing all the talking, but she was up there with him."

Rufus looked at the phone. "Says her role is Senior Business Developer. Hang on—there's a Twitter account linked. Her last tweet was from this morning. 'Back in NYC and this year's MoDe promises to be the best yet!'"

"Hold on, do you still have that convention program?"

"Yeah." Rufus set his phone and food aside, went to his pile of winter clothing, and tugged free the severely bent program from his sweatshirt pocket. He offered it to Sam while sitting again.

"So that panel was… 'Tactical Vehicles: Challenges, Opportunities, Sustainment, Modification. Moderated by Delmer Jolly (Conasauga Solutions) and Evangeline Ridgeway (Conasauga Solutions). Col. Leslie Bridges, 194th Armored Brigade, Respondent.' What the actual fuck?"

Rufus was scrubbing his head with one hand and could feel his shock of hair sticking on end. "I have no idea what any of that means."

"That woman calls herself a business developer, but my guess is she's just doing sales. The company guys say, 'Ra ra, look what we did.' And the salespeople say, 'This is how what we did can help you.' And the colonel says, 'Here's the thing they did, and it's great, so we definitely need more tanks.' The usual circle-jerk."

The uncertainty Rufus felt as he tried to wrap his brain around the workings of Big Money and Big Government and big everything—it was the only lame adjective he could think of—was making him break out into a self-conscious flush. "There was that accident—Stonefish. And the company that'd been involved was Conasauga. And now that company is at an expo here in the city, probably pushing similar gear? And Shareed Baker tracked you down to sell information about Stonefish, but is now dead. And my cop-daddy is asking about Conasauga's hot sales lady. Did I miss anything?"

"Your cop-daddy," Sam said in an undertone. More loudly, he said, "And Lew's here. I know you think I've got tunnel vision, but I don't think that's a coincidence. Shareed said his name. He'd just made captain when

Stonefish happened. The shit didn't stick to him, and now, a couple years later, here he is: at a Conasauga panel, where they're talking about how successful the Army's partnership with Conasauga has been, all the benefits of Conasauga's tactical vehicles, that kind of shit."

"We should go back to the expo tomorrow. I can leave Dr. Donna a message and let her know I have to miss my session." Rufus grabbed his phone.

"I don't want you missing your session," Sam said.

"Well, you're not going to the Javits alone."

"We can do both, can't we? What time is your appointment?"

Rufus hesitated. "Two o'clock."

"Great. We'll try the convention in the morning, break for lunch, get you to your appointment, and then see where we're at."

Rufus set his phone down. A hint of attitude came out as he murmured, "You're so thoughtful."

"It's important, Rufus."

"I know. I love poking at old and festering wounds." Rufus put the lid on his food and pushed the container aside. "Never mind. I was just trying to be helpful."

"Thank you for being willing to change your plans, but we can make it work."

Rufus collected two of the three food containers and stood. He brought them to the fridge, tossed the takeout on the mostly bare top shelf, shut the door, then leaned back against it. He stared at Sam, still seated on the floor, dumplings now seemingly forgotten. "Can I ask you something?"

Sam nodded.

"Are you happy? I mean, with me."

"Because I got mad about Lew?"

"I'm really asking."

"Yes. I wouldn't mind not having Pauly as a neighbor, but other than that…." He shrugged.

Rufus looked toward the left wall at the mention of his perpetually drunk and stoned neighbor in 4C, who didn't sound like he was home at the moment. "So you like living with me?"

"What are you asking me?" Sam got up and moved over to the sink in the tiny kitchen. He ran the water, stared at it for a moment, and turned it off. "If you're asking me if I'm happy with you, the answer is yes. I love you. If you're asking me if I like living here, I mean, Jesus, Rufus. Does anyone like living in Manhattan?"

Rufus winced. Without realizing it, Sam had just confirmed what he'd been sensing, fearing, *dreading*. Into the quiet, Rufus answered, "I do."

"Of course you do."

"You think it's bad that I like it here?"

"No. Not—" The light from the low-wattage bulb left shadows on Sam's face. "I mean, this place works for you. Of course you like it."

Pushing off the fridge, Rufus said, "Yeah."

"What does that mean?"

"It means, I think you're full of shit."

"Excuse me?"

Rufus had been halfway to the bathroom before he stopped and turned around. "I only like Manhattan because Manhattan is all I know, is what you want to say. And I think it bothers you that I'm not—I don't know—worldly. That if we left the city I wouldn't be able to survive."

"Christ, Rufus. Where did you get that from?"

"It's true," he protested, walking back to Sam. "What the fuck would I do for a living if we ever left? I have no education, no job experience, my skills include lockpicking and petty theft, I mean, what the fuck. And so you stay here because, maybe you do love me, but mostly because you know if you left, I wouldn't. I couldn't."

Sam shook his head. "What am I supposed to say to that?"

Rufus wiped his face on his shirt. "A few weeks ago, I told Dr. Donna that when I feel like shit, when I can't get out of bed or I can't breathe, I always think about you. Thinking about you makes me feel a little better—a little more sane. Then I started worrying that that's probably not healthy and I should figure out a better coping method because it puts too much expectation on you. That thought turned into disappointing you, which snowballed into you being unhappy with me, and now I can't stop thinking about how I'm probably making you miserable because I'm being selfish—asking you to live in a place with too much noise and too many people when I know you actively despise both.

"I just... I don't want to go to therapy tomorrow. I don't want to talk about how scared I am to lose the one good thing in my life, but how it feels inevitable and I should sabotage my relationship now so it hurts less later."

The radiator gurgled. Sam wiped his mouth. Then he came across the room and wrapped Rufus in a hug. "You're not making me miserable. I love you. I don't know what to say about the rest of it; we'll figure it out."

Rufus put his arms around Sam's neck and said against his shoulder, "I thought therapy was supposed to feel good, but every step forward feels like three steps back."

"Maybe every step forward is three sideways." Sam smiled against the side of Rufus's head. "That would be about right for us."

"Sounds like a dance move white boys do at prom."

"Good God," Sam said and huffed a laugh. Then he

turned Rufus's face up and kissed him.

"I'm sorry. You've got enough to think about. I didn't mean to let all the batshit crazy out."

"We carry each other's batshit crazy." Sam tugged on the hem of Rufus's shirt. "That's kind of the whole point."

Rufus smiled. It felt a little out-of-body, but he hadn't had a panic attack. A few months ago, hell, a few weeks ago, he probably would have. He molded himself to Sam's body, breathed when he breathed. "I thought that was some weird kink we shared."

CHAPTER
ELEVEN

The next day, the Javits was even busier. People thronged the atrium, shouting to be heard over each other, with enough cologne and perfume in the air to make Sam think a brothel had exploded inside a Bath & Body Works. It was so overwhelming that he barely felt his phone buzz.

He didn't recognize the number; he answered on the third ring.

"Good morning! May I please speak to Samuel Auden?"

"Who is this?"

"Good morning, Mr. Auden! My name is Sara, and I'm a student at Columbia Law School! I'm calling today because I'm volunteering for the Restore Our America

Committee, and I wanted to ask for your support in bringing back the glory of our great country by donating to Congresswoman Nasta's reelection campaign!"

"Pass," Sam said.

Sara was working on what felt like her fifteenth exclamation mark, saying, "Thank you anyway! While I've got you on the line, could you confirm your contact—"

He hit End.

Rufus was fixing his beanie while watching Sam. "Who was that?"

"Who the fuck knows? She needs a fucking Quaalude, whoever she is. That election isn't for almost a year." Sam glanced around. No sign of Brady, although it was impossible to check every face in the crowded space. If Lew had his guard dog on patrol, Sam guessed it would be downstairs, in the exhibition hall. Which, of course, was where they needed to start their search for Evangeline Ridgeway. He let out a sigh.

Rufus lowered his voice to a false baritone and mimicked Sam's "Pass." He caught Sam's stare and tried to pass off a smile that was anything but innocent.

Sam rolled his eyes and started throwing elbows to clear a path to the escalator. He held his own pretty well; the only setback was the old lady who got him in the knee with her cane, but it had been a dirty hit—she'd cheated and gotten him when he wasn't looking.

The crowd thinned as they rode down to the exhibition hall. Sam adjusted the badge hanging around his neck. "Do you still have the program from yesterday?"

"*Oui, mon capitaine.*" Rufus yanked the program free from his sweatshirt. He worked the wrinkles out a little before offering it.

Sam flipped through the day's events. "She's not on the schedule today, but it shouldn't be too hard to find her.

Once you take all the old white men out of the equation, there are like six people left."

"Sausage fest is the term you're looking for."

"God," Sam said as he stepped off the escalator. "Now I've got that in my head."

They moved around the perimeter of the hall. Booths and tables in orderly rows filled the center of the large room. And while the people manning the booths and tables looked bright-eyed and bushy-tailed, ready to explain how their laser or their railgun or their new bullet jacket would be the perfect thing for Iraq or Afghanistan or, hell, Detroit if it came to that, the men and women circulating through the hall scarcely seemed to notice the displays and the charts and the catchy banners. The people at this convention—and at a hundred other conventions like this—weren't there for the booths and the banners. They were there for the other people like them. So Sam watched faces. And he inspected the Conasauga booth, where a young woman with dimples and a paisley scarf around her neck was smiling and nodding at passersby and looking giddy at the mere possibility of a chance to talk about tactical vehicles. But he didn't see Evangeline Ridgeway.

"Ok," he muttered at the end of their circuit. "Now what?"

Rufus snagged the program back from Sam, moved against a wall where he'd be out of the way, and flipped through the pages. "You said she wasn't on the schedule, but maybe she's rubbing shoulders at a bar or something." He took out his phone and checked the time. "Or having coffee, I should say. Hey. Check Twitter—see if she posted anything patriotic that might also suggest a location."

With a grimace, Sam opened Twitter and found Ridgeway's handle. She had retweeted several posts from pro-military accounts—including one from a veterans advocate Sam actually recognized. She'd also included an angry tweet about her latte because it was too milky, and she'd tagged the coffeeshop in the kind of petty vindictiveness that social media rewarded. And then, from a couple of hours before, a tweet that said *Looking forward to @urgenta's presentation on their THUNDER platform and updates. Keeping America Safe!*

"You know what?" Sam said as he flashed the message at Rufus. "I think she would have done great under Hitler."

Rufus made a face but then started flipping through the program again. "She sounds like a real—ah, Urgenta. Panel ends in about ten minutes. Man, these people start protecting America before I'm even out of bed. Did you want to try and catch her afterward?"

"It's worth a shot."

They used the postage-stamp-sized map in the program to head toward the room where the panel was being held. People were already starting to sneak out of this hour's sessions, which meant that the hall was filling up again. A couple of guys threw Sam and Rufus second glances. Maybe they were closet cases. Hell, maybe they were out-and-out homos. But the back of Sam's neck prickled, and he remembered his brush with Brady, and he wondered how many people had been given their description since yesterday afternoon.

After two wrong tries, they found the Urgenta panel as it was ending. The double doors stood open, and a throng of bored-looking—and slightly sweaty—people were pouring out into the hallway. Sam scanned faces. Rufus broke away from his side without comment, weaving his way through the exiting crowd, and vanishing into the sea of people on the opposite side of the Urgenta doors.

Sam opened his mouth to call after him, and then he spotted Evangeline. He hadn't paid much attention to her the day before when he had been reacting to the shock of seeing Lew, but he recognized the shape of her face, the plastic smile. She wore a simple navy suit that looked good on her and managed to look expensive while still being understated. Her brown hair was long and artfully curled—Sam didn't want to think about the wake-up call time for hair like that. She was talking to a young man who stumbled while Sam was watching; he was trying to look down her shirt. Ah, young love.

"Ms. Ridgeway?" Sam called and fought his way through the river of bodies.

Her head came up. Dark eyes focused on him, assessed, tried to catalog. Cold eyes. File not found.

"I'm sorry," she said as people streamed around Sam with varying looks of irritation. One older man even harrumphed. "Have we met?"

"Not officially," Sam said. "Could I have a moment of your time?"

"Excuse me, Anson," she said.

Anson was still trying to see her tatas, and he didn't seem to realize what was happening until she had already stepped away.

Sam followed her a few yards down the hall to a spot where the crowd thinned. Rufus was coming up in the opposite direction, and although Sam didn't know what the redhead was planning, he figured it was sneaky. He positioned himself so that Evangeline had to turn to face him, with her back now to Rufus.

"I'm sorry, Mr.—"

"Auden. Sam Auden."

Her expression remained pleasantly blank.

"I wanted to talk to you about Shareed Baker."

This time the computer eyes found and accessed the file right away. Whatever was on the hard drive, it didn't make Evangeline happy, but the rest of her face stayed rigidly congenial. "Who?"

"You know who."

Rufus had shaken out the program, raised it up like he meant to read from it, then bumped Evangeline's right shoulder as he stepped past. "Oops," he said automatically, not stopping as he continued at a leisurely pace back toward the exhibition hall.

"Excuse me," Evangeline called after him, but Rufus didn't look back.

"Shareed Baker," Sam said.

When she looked back at him, she'd locked down her expression again. "I'm sorry, I don't know who you are, and I don't know who Shareed Baker is. You must have me confused with someone else."

"Really?" Sam asked. "That's not what the NYPD thinks. Do you want to explain why your name came up in an investigation of Shareed Baker's death?"

The delay was fractional, but it was there. The question had been a body blow. But then Evangeline had the plastic smile back into place, and she was shaking her head as she said, "But you're not with the police, are you? You would have told me if you were. Goodbye, Mr. Auden."

She held herself a little too stiffly as she clicked away on her heels, and her voice was a little too bright as she called down the hall, "Douglas St. John, stop right there, you wicked old man. You owe me a coffee!"

And Douglas St. John, who looked like he was already a couple of pacemakers deep, waved a liver-spotted hand and smiled a DentaWhite smile.

Once Evangeline and Douglas St. John had begun walking, Rufus re-appeared around the corner. He moved on long legs back to Sam, holding up what looked to be a hotel keycard still in the paper sleeve. Rufus had a shit-eating grin on his face.

"I was prepared for anything," he began. "What was

she gonna have? A clutch? A tote? A purse is a guy's best friend—those flap ones with the magnetic button. Do you know how quickly I can open one of those and snag a wallet?" Rufus didn't let Sam answer before holding up two fingers. "Two seconds. Two fucking seconds. So like I said, I was ready. But when I saw you walking with her— no purse, no nothing—I thought, what kind of lady isn't carrying *something*. Then I saw the square outline on her thigh and realized she had pockets—shallow ones, too— and anyway, I got her hotel card."

Sam blinked his way through the onslaught of information. Then he said, "Good job?"

Rufus took out his phone, copied the name of the hotel from the envelope's decal, then said, "Thirty-Seventh and Tenth. Looks like they're partners with a vegan Japanese restaurant too." He put the phone away. "I don't know who would eat vegan sushi, but there you go."

The exposition hall was emptying again, the outgoing tide of bodies as the next round of panels began. Evangeline had disappeared into another room, which meant, Sam hoped, that she'd be at the expo for at least another hour. He nodded toward the escalator and said, "Let's go."

The Savoy-Hell's Kitchen was a newish-looking building with a white-brick veneer and enormous windows. Even in the scummy winter light, chrome trim glinted and flashed when the clouds shifted. It looked like the kind of place midlevel executives would hire midlevel hookers, presumably while midlevel pimps waited in midlevel sedans. It wasn't what Sam had expected from Evangeline Ridgeway, and he wondered who was footing the bill. The Army, maybe? God knows they'd love a place like the Savoy-Hell's Kitchen.

Inside, the lobby consisted of carpet squares in

muted color patterns, modernish seating with easy-wash upholstery, and the kind of blond wood furniture that interior decorators seemed to think screamed civilization. A few solitary people were spaced throughout the room, two men and a woman, all of them absorbed in their devices. To the right, an opening connected with the hotel bar, where the lights were dimmed even in the late morning and the dark wood and tinted glass suggested the kind of sophistication that involved olives and, at the end of the night, a case of crabs. The front desk stood at the far end, and the white boy who was working the desk had locs and the smirk of a guy used to getting some without really trying. He was on his phone—presumably in the midst of arranging to get some later, to judge by that smirk—and didn't look up when Sam and Rufus passed him on the way to the elevator.

Sam had just pressed the Up button when he heard a man say behind him, "Trouble finding a cab, Colonel?"

Rocking back on his heels, Sam waited a beat until he thought he could be casual. Then he glanced over his shoulder.

A man in a navy suit and wool overcoat had just come through the revolving door; Sam recognized him as the person Lew had been talking to—arguing with—when Sam had spotted him the day before. He was solidly built, balding, with a small mouth and teeth that made Sam think of a rat. Another man, older, was rising from where he'd been sitting in the lobby. He wore his white hair in a side part, slicked back in a way that suggested 1983, and he wore money like cologne; he looked like he had probably been best friends with Reagan. Sam recognized him, now that he turned his full attention to the man—he had also been on the stage. The one Evangeline had called Del. Some sort of executive, if Sam remembered correctly, with Conasauga.

The man who must be Colonel Leslie Bridges, if the

convention program was accurate, was out of uniform. He pulled off his overcoat, glanced around, and said, "I was finalizing arrangements. As I said on the phone, I think we've reached the end of our road together."

Del made a moue. "Let's be civilized about this. A drink? Maybe I can change your mind."

Bridges glanced at the bar.

"It's five o'clock somewhere," Del said with a boardroom laugh, and he gestured for the colonel to lead the way.

The elevator dinged, and the doors rattled open as the two men passed through the opening into the bar.

Sam shot a look at the elevator. Then at the bar.

Rufus held the elevator door when it began to shut. "Hey," he said, voice low. "Did you want to go up or listen to Frick and Frack over there?"

"The bar is pretty much empty; they'll spot us as soon as we walk in."

Rufus slapped the door a second time and the elevator let out an obnoxious beep. He peered around Sam's shoulder and then with a nod of his chin in the direction of the bar, said, "Look at that stand by the entrance—all those tourism pamphlets. We might be able to hear them from there."

The elevator doors began to rattle shut. Sam caught them. They rattled open. Then, with a frustrated, grunt, he nodded.

OFFICIAL NYC TOURIST GUIDE

WHEN MANHATTAN COMES TO MANHATTAN: WHAT TO DO IN NYC IF YOU'RE FROM KANSAS

TIMES SQUARE - A VD SUCCESS STORY

Ok, Sam added that last part in his head.

There were pamphlets on the Empire State Building,

the Statue of Liberty, the MOMA, the Met, even on visiting the Macy's flagship store. Sam scanned them all, occasionally plucking one from the rack and opening it, folding it backward along the crease like he was really invested in learning about the Alice statue. But his attention was focused on the bar.

Rufus had been right; he could hear what was happening. Some of it, anyway. The clink of glass. Movement. Low voices. But not enough to make out—

"And I've done everything you've asked!"

That part came through clearly enough, Del's words delivered in a low, angry voice that carried to the lobby.

The colonel's response was muffled, but it sounded calm and self-assured.

"You can't," Del whisper-shouted. "We had a deal."

This time, the colonel's response was audible: "And we both got what we wanted."

"No, I—"

"Don't press me on this, Del. I don't like problems. I don't like loose threads. Do you know what I do to loose threads?" The colonel's voice was moving toward them now. Rufus yanked on Sam's sleeve, and Sam let himself be led away, but he could still make out the colonel's final words. "I tie them off. We aren't going to talk again."

Rufus was pressing the Up button as the colonel emerged from the bar. The bell dinged. The doors rattled open. Because, of course, the damn thing was still on this floor. The colonel glanced over, and his gaze settled on Sam and Rufus.

Rufus yanked on Sam's arm again, and Sam stumbled onto the elevator after him.

"Fuck," Sam muttered as the doors clattered shut. "Fuck, fuck, fuck."

Rufus jabbed the 6 button with his thumb before

looking at Sam. "I grew up on the street—I know what the fuck a loose thread implies—but should a military guy be talking like that?"

"Of course not. That's some shady shit. That guy, Del, he was running the Conasauga presentation with Evangeline. Lew was there. So was the colonel. Shareed and Lew. Shareed and Evangeline. This is a fucking rat's nest."

"Vipers," Rufus corrected. "They all sound like a bunch of snakes." The doors opened on the sixth floor and Rufus checked the keycard envelope. "612."

The hallway was pleasantly neutral, well lit, and empty. It felt surreal. When Rufus tried the card, the lock on 612 flashed green, and a motor whirred. Rufus leaned into the door, and it opened.

It had the faintly dry smell of forced-air heating as well as something lighter and floral—the perfume Evangeline wore, which was doubtless expensive. The room was dark, with the blackout curtains drawn so that only a sliver of light passed through a gap where they met. Sam caught the light switch, and a few dim yellow overheads came to life, revealing the king bed, the dresser, the television, the armchair, the desk with mid-executive-level accessories, like a vinyl blotter and a lamp. A leather portfolio case was closed on the desk. Her suitcase, zippered shut, occupied a stand near the bed. The closet door stood ajar, revealing two dresses—both black—hanging from the rod.

"Split up?" Sam asked.

Rufus said, "I'm not looking through a lady's unmentionables." And he moved toward the window, desk, and armchair corner.

Sam had barely unzipped the suitcase before Rufus called his name.

"Hey, Sam. I might be the savviest shit east of the Hudson." Rufus was carefully holding up the desk blotter with his thumb and index finger while pointing at a single sheet of paper underneath. When Sam came toward him, Rufus said, "Please agree and call me savvy. Or smart. Actually, there're a lot of good adjectives starting with 'S.'"

"Fine. You're savvy. You're smart. You're a snarky, snarly, sexy pile of trouble. What do you have?"

"I don't know, but it looks very official."

Rolling his eyes, Sam snagged the paper. He scanned it. Then he read it again.

"This is a PR release. About Stonefish. What the actual fuck?"

Rufus asked, "Why would she have a PR release with her for something that happened a long time ago?"

"'Conasauga Solutions is pleased to announce the performance and operability ratings of JLTV models M1279.S and M1280.S (Project STONEFISH).' Jesus Christ, they make it sound like they're winning J.D. Power awards. Let's see. Army loves them. Big order coming. Public unveiling of Stonefish models to be attended by—" He stopped. "The rest of it's missing."

Rufus raised his eyebrows. "What do you mean, missing?"

Sam displayed the page, where the press release had been photocopied. It cut off abruptly after the mention of the public unveiling.

"Ain't that a bitch. There's space on the page... I wonder why it got cut."

"I don't think it was an accident."

Rufus met Sam's gaze a second time. "So someone sent this to Evangeline? As what... a threat?"

"I don't know. But it must mean something to her, because she kept it."

"Sam?" Rufus was staring at the opposite side of the

paper. "What's this on the back?"

Sam turned the page over, glanced at the series of numbers, and displayed it for Rufus. "An account number?"

"Bank account number," Rufus corrected. "What's this—oh—SWIFT code, isn't it?"

"Do we know anybody who wanted to sell information about Stonefish?"

Rufus's shoulders sagged. "Shareed," he murmured.

When they left the room, a housekeeping cart was parked two doors down, and from within the lighted room came the sounds of rustling cotton and footsteps. The elevator carried them to the lobby, where the clerk was trying to (somewhat) discreetly snap a dick pic under the front desk before he noticed them, at which point he banged his knee, yanked on something, and made a shrill noise.

"Zipper," Sam muttered.

The lobby had emptied while they were upstairs, and as Sam headed for the revolving door, he had halfway convinced himself that he'd imagined the colonel spotting them earlier.

Over his shoulder, he said to Rufus, "We have to talk to Lew, obviously, which means back to the convention center. Public is better for now, I think, but how do you want to do it?"

Rufus had stopped following a few feet back, and when Sam stopped and looked at him, Rufus pointed toward the almost empty bar. "What about talking to that Del guy first?"

CHAPTER
TWELVE

"Give me that press release."

With a raised eyebrow, Sam held it out. "What are we going to say?"

Rufus snatched the paper while echoing, "We? *We* aren't saying anything. *I'm* saying something. You stay here and look pretty."

"Excuse me?"

"I know you heard me." Rufus smirked before pivoting on his heel and strolling into the dimly lit bar. Delmer Jolly sat alone, tapping at his phone in one hand, the other holding a tumbler of rich amber liquid. It was probably scotch, Rufus decided. Scotch felt like a rich man's drink. He pulled out the chair beside Del and made a show of sitting down—just to annoy the guy a little. "How's it hangin'?" Rufus asked.

Del arched one trimmed white eyebrow. "Good morning."

Rufus shrugged. "It's a morning. So, you visiting the city?"

"I'm sorry, do I know you?"

"My manners. You'd think I was raised by an underage hooker." Rufus held a hand out. "Rufus Smith."

Del considered his hand. Then he moved his phone and glass closer. "I'm sorry, Mr. Smith. I'm flattered, of course. But I'm not interested. No offense." He smiled thinly. "You understand."

Rufus lowered his hand a fraction before blurting, "What? Oh no, no, no. I'm not into older guys. I mean—a few years is fine, but you're in a completely different generational bracket." Unfolding the paper, Rufus put it on the tabletop, but with a palm firmly over it so it couldn't be snatched. "JLTV models M1279.S and M1280.S," he read. "Wow. That's a mouthful. I'll just call it Stonefish. So it was a big success, huh?"

This time, both eyebrows went up, and it looked like Del was fighting the urge to lean forward to inspect the paper. "That's a nice bit of showmanship. I'm supposed to wonder what you have."

"But you are wondering, aren't you?" Rufus met Del's steady gaze with one of his shit-eating grins.

On the other side of the tinted glass, traffic ebbed and flowed. Light glanced off a taxi's windows, but it looked gray and matte through the treated glass. A horn blared. It sounded like it was a mile off.

Del pocketed his phone. He sipped his scotch, and as the glass clicked against the table, he said, "I assume Stonefish is supposed to mean something to me. Why don't you tell me what you want, Mr. Smith, and quit wasting my time?"

Rufus smoothed the paper a few times, enough for the action to hold Del's attention, then he carefully folded the top down so that the string of numbers on the backside was visible. "Why don't you start with Shareed Baker and finish with why she'd want you and your sales lady to have her bank account and routing number." He looked at Del, and with feigned ignorance, said, "Weird."

"I don't know anyone by that name, and I don't know what you're talking about. I'd like you to leave now."

"Oh, sure, sure. I have to call my cop-daddy with the NYPD anyway."

"I'm sure he'll be interested in—what was it you said?" Del started to rise. "Good luck to you."

"That sure lit a fire under your ass. First you wanted *me* to leave, but then maybe I mention the cops, maybe I mention they're investigating a dead woman found in her hotel room yesterday, maybe I even mention said dead woman had a financial interest in you and your expo buddies, and suddenly you've gotta run?"

"A dead woman," Del said. He still had one hand on the table. His fingertips were bloodless. "What are you talking about?"

Rufus narrowed his eyes a little. His tone shifted from something playful and cocky to somber as he answered, "Shareed Baker called the Javits over and over just before she died. She died after having left Evangeline Ridgeway with what amounted to blackmail. That's what I'm talking about."

"I don't know what I could possibly have to do with—"

"Yes, you do. That's why you want to get the fuck out of here."

Del's lips pressed together, pinched and white. With what looked like a great deal of effort, he peeled his hand from the table in a slow, controlled movement. "I was on a Conasauga jet yesterday morning with the rest of my staff. Whatever happened to that poor woman, whoever she is, I had nothing to do with it. Goodbye, Mr. Smith. If you contact me again, you'll hear from my lawyer."

Rufus raised a hand to the side of his head and saluted Del as the older man left the bar. He waited a full minute before helping himself to the rest of Del's mostly untouched drink, and then walked out. Rufus was coughing and thumping his chest as he returned to Sam. "That bartender pours strong."

"What'd he say?"

Rufus finished clearing his throat. "He denied everything. The only thing I could get out of him that wasn't *I have no idea what you're talking about*, was that he was on a Conasauga jet yesterday morning—when Shareed died."

Sam's hands tightened and then relaxed. "That makes sense. If he was involved—if—he would have sent someone else to do it. It doesn't tell us anything one way or another."

"It tells us Conasauga has a jet," Rufus replied. "I'd be curious to find out how many of the folks at MoDe were on that jet at the same time."

"Sure. It's worth finding out."

Rufus scratched the stubble on his chin. "Would Lew have been on that jet, you think?"

"No."

"We should find out where he was yesterday morning." Rufus hastily continued, "But before you kill Lew, we have to consider the fact that this press release was in Evangeline's room, and that Del jumped to alibi himself when I mentioned Shareed was dead. Whatever's going on is messier than what I expected. We need to *talk* to Lew."

Sam opened his mouth, but he must have changed what he was going to say because he hesitated. "So let's talk to him. Move things along so we can get to the killing part."

"Don't turn into the Incredible Hulk just yet." Rufus started for the revolving door before stopping so abruptly that he nearly tripped over his own two feet.

Lew Frazer, still big, still built, and still bronze, had just entered the hotel. His commanding presence swallowed up the air around him, and if Rufus hadn't already known his background, he'd have definitely pegged the guy as military or at least a Suit at one of the many alphabet agencies.

Speaking of suits—Brady Ellsworth stood behind Lew like an obedient little gremlin—and two more men Rufus didn't recognize completed the entourage.

Rufus backpedaled into Sam.

Sam glanced around. "Mother. Fucker. Frazer, good, you just saved me the trouble of finding your ass so I can put you in the ground."

Rufus turned slightly and dug his elbow into Sam's chest while hissing, "Stop it."

Lew flashed an easy smile. "Auden. It's been a while. I've been looking for you. Let's go for a ride."

"We're good, actually," Rufus answered for Sam, who felt so taut under his touch that Rufus half expected him to snap like a broken rubber band. "Those taxis cost an arm and a leg these days."

The look from Lew took him in and dismissed him, all in an instant. Brady, on the other hand, was staring murder at Rufus. Apparently he hadn't forgotten round one.

"There's no reason we need to make this difficult," Lew said to Sam. "You show up, you start poking your nose in, well, it makes people uncomfortable. So let's go for a ride, and we'll figure out how everybody walks away from this happy."

"What did I tell you, Lew?" Sam asked. He had a hand on Rufus's shoulder, and he was trying to move him from his path. "What did I say?"

"You were upset. You and that kid were butt—" Lew's smile had a frat boy's guilty charm. "Close. I didn't hold it against you."

"I told you if I ever saw you again, there wouldn't be enough left of you to bury."

Then he shoved Rufus aside and launched himself at Lew.

Rufus stumbled and came just short of toppling over the brochure stand. He needed to put on weight so he couldn't be flung around like a damn leaf in a hurricane. He turned, saw Sam grab Lew, saw Brady clench his fists, and then Rufus threw himself on the bomb ready to detonate.

"Sam, stop!" Rufus wormed his way in between Sam and Lew and tried to push his boyfriend back, which was akin to pushing a brick wall.

"Hey!" the white guy with locs at the front desk shouted. He held the desk phone in one hand and was shaking the receiver at them. "Are you all fuckin' kidding me? Don't make me call the cops."

"Back the fuck away," Rufus said sternly to Sam.

"What you did to Went," Sam shouted, "what you did to Shareed, I'm going to make you pay for it, Frazer!"

"Chill out," Rufus snapped. "The last fucking thing I want to do is call Erik from a jail cell."

"Sorry about the disturbance," Lew called to the front desk clerk. "It was a misunderstanding."

"Fuck your misunderstandings," Sam shouted, still trying to get past Rufus. "And fuck you."

Brady took a step forward, like he was more than

happy to meet Sam halfway.

"*Sam*," Rufus said again. He took ahold of Sam's biceps and gave him a hard shake. "Stop. I'm not bailing you out." He said to Brady, "And unless you want to piss blood for the rest of the week, step off my ass, buddy."

Brady's expression darkened, but he stopped moving forward.

Rufus finally spoke to Lew. "So when'd you get into town?"

This time, Lew seemed to take Rufus in as though seeing him for the first time. He smirked at Sam. "You didn't always like them so skinny. He's got a little more pep than Went, though, doesn't he?"

Sam's answer was a rumble in his chest. At least, for the moment, he'd stopped trying to thrust Rufus to one side.

"We'll have that talk another time, Auden. Figure out how everybody walks away from this with what they want. See you around."

Rufus shifted, moving so that he always stood in front of Sam as Lew, Brady, and the Dingbat Twins made for the bank of elevators. He waited until the elevator rattled opened, the party stepped inside, and then disappeared. He turned and gave Sam a final shove. "What the fuck is wrong with you?"

Sam glared past him, his gaze fixed on the street.

"Don't ignore me. We agreed to talk to him. But the second you made eye contact you went feral." Rufus swore, put his hands on his hips, and after a beat, asked Sam, "Are you going to do this every time? Because we're gonna cross paths with Lew again."

After a moment, he managed, "Maybe." He cleared his throat. "I don't know."

CHAPTER
THIRTEEN

When they stepped out of the hotel, the city was like sandpaper on raw nerves. Cars alternated between accelerating at full speed and then stopping suddenly in a screech of brakes. A FedEx truck was double parked, prompting an old woman in a Lincoln to lay on the horn. A guy with light brown skin and Jheri curls wore nothing but a t-shirt and baby carrier in which a Beagle was riding, glancing around and barking loudly enough to compete with the horn.

Sam remembered the feel of Lew's shirt, the cloth between his fingers.

A white kid on a skateboard whizzed past, clipping Sam with his elbow.

"Jesus Christ," Sam muttered and sucked in a breath. "Can I get out of this fuck-hole for five seconds?"

Rufus shot Sam a critical look, but all he asked was "Want lunch?"

Sam nodded.

They ended up in a taqueria called Diabla, which was set down from the sidewalk. The peeling paint on the door and the ancient soaped letters on the windows spelling T CO T DAY were not promising, but inside, the air smelled like seared pork and cilantro and onion, and the warmth and relative humidity made it feel like walking into a steam bath. While Rufus secured a two-top against the wall, Sam ordered, and by the time he'd paid, his tray was ready. He carried it to the table, passed Rufus an empty foam cup, and said, "I got everything. I'm not—I'm not exactly in a place to make decisions."

"It's fine," Rufus said, sounding like he was trying very hard to not be short. He went to the counter with the cup, asked for it to be filled with Pepsi, and returned to the table. "You know," he began with a forced casualness. "If you tell them you don't like ice because it hurts your teeth, you get extra soda." He sat, tugged his beanie off, and tossed it onto the tabletop.

Sam bit into a taco. He wasn't sure what the meat was. It was brown, anyway. And the onions added a nice flavor. Too much cilantro. After a moment, when Rufus hadn't sucked up half the food like a human vacuum cleaner, Sam nudged the tray toward him.

Rufus obediently took one of the tacos and downed it in two bites. Seemingly in-sync with Sam's own culinary thoughts, he said, "I read a book that claimed there's a gene responsible for why so many people say cilantro tastes like soap. OR6-something... 6A2, maybe?" Rufus grabbed a second taco, took a bite, and said, "Thankfully, my OR-whatever works just fine."

"Are we not going to talk about Lew? Is that the plan?"

Rufus chewed and swallowed. He stared at Sam for a long minute before saying, "I don't know. I wasn't the one who tried to assault him. Can you talk about him without seeing red?"

"I don't know what you want me to say. I told him what I'd do to him. There's no doubt in my mind what happened: the colonel spotted us, called Lew, and sicced him on us. Lew knew what I was going to do, and he came anyway. That's on him."

"I want you to use your imagination for a minute."

Sam raised his eyebrows.

"Pretend I'm in a full-blown panic attack," Rufus started.

"Ok."

"And you love me—remember that. Now, I just said everything you did. Am I freaking out, or is there something there worth listening to?"

For a moment, Sam considered this. He set down a half-eaten taco. "It would be hard to know. You're not always wrong when you're panicking, but it's hard to follow your reasoning, and you're often too upset to see alternatives."

"Yeah, sometimes. I know. So what would you say to me?"

The plastic straw tore easily, and Sam peeled it into strips. "I don't know."

Rufus let out a sigh as he leaned back in his chair. "I guess this is me having trouble with *your* reasoning."

"What part?"

"All of it, maybe. I used to think, for a street rat, I was pretty smart. But being around all these people at MoDe—I don't know if I'm ignorant or just plain stupid. Can you tell me why you think the two of us are a threat worth calling in backup over?"

"Because of Stonefish. Because Lew knew I didn't believe the bullshit story they told about Went. Because he must have known Shareed would contact me and tell me what she found. I don't know all the pieces, Rufus, but they're all involved in it, and Lew didn't show up at this hotel by accident."

Rufus picked up a third taco. "Was Went more than a friend?"

"He's dead."

"That wasn't my question, Sam."

"He was... Christ, I don't know. He wasn't my boyfriend. We didn't even have sex. But he was sweet, and he—I don't know." Sam struggled, working his jaw. "I cared about him. He wasn't cut out for the Army, but he worked damn hard, and if he'd lived, yeah, maybe." He pushed the tray away again. "Does that help with your line of reasoning?"

Rufus shrugged. "You don't need to keep it a secret."

"And now you know. Can we talk about something important now? Like what we're going to do about this mess?"

Wryly, Rufus suggested, "Run away to Nebraska?"

"Wouldn't that be a dream. Lew's a lot of things, but he doesn't make empty threats. If he says he's going to come after us, he's going to come after us. We need to figure out how we're going to handle it when he does." With a grunt, Sam gathered their trash. "What are we going to do now?"

"I think we should try to find out if Del was telling the truth about not yet being in the city when Shareed died. At least it'd narrow our focus a bit."

"Right," Sam said. "Here we go."

CHAPTER
FOURTEEN

The books piled onto the sale carts outside the front doors of The Strand had always been Rufus's favorites to dig through. He'd long ago figured out that those books, and their extremely niche subject matter, were typically hard sells with the general public, and so for very little investment, Rufus could learn a lot. And sure, he could learn the exact same things for free at the library, but sometimes picking through the once lovingly used, now abandoned, books felt sort of like he was saving them from the certain fate of ending up in a dumpster.

Rufus knew he was actually projecting his own feelings of inadequacy, his own fears of worthlessness—surely he'd have had a better childhood if he were lovable—and he knew it wasn't healthy behavior, but he couldn't help anthropomorphizing used books. After all, titles like *Mathematical Fractals in Everyday Life*, *History of Irish Ballads*, *New York Ghost Stories*, and *101 Gays of the Nineteenth Century* had been some of his best friends—his only friends—before meeting Jake.

Before meeting Sam.

Rufus glanced up from his phone to study Sam seated across the table, the empty taco tray still between them. Sam had come into his life like a wrecking ball, to borrow from Miley Cyrus, and Rufus had found in him a friend. Someone who had cared about his well-being, had wanted to spend free time with him, talk with him, and Rufus had wanted to do the very same in return. Even with the somewhat rocky evolution of their relationship, and the fact that they were now romantically involved, which came with all-new complexities and complications, it didn't negate how they'd begun, didn't negate that Sam had believed Rufus when he'd needed it the most.

Rufus didn't understand their situation, would have given his left nut to pretend Shareed and Lew and Del Jolly and Colonel Bridges didn't exist so he could go home and curl up in bed with the most eclectic book in his collection, but Sam needed support.

Sam needed someone to believe him.

Rufus had a real friend now, and his real friend needed him.

"Conasauga Solutions definitely has a private plane," Rufus said, looking back down at the Facebook business page open on his phone. He swiped through photos with corporate jargon descriptions before stopping on one of the plane parked on a tarmac with half a dozen rich-looking people standing beside its staircase. He pinched the screen to zoom in. "I'm hoping to find some sort of identification. You can pop that into a website that tracks private planes, you know."

"Even if he's telling the truth, it doesn't mean he wasn't behind what happened to Shareed. He can make a phone call from a plane just like anywhere else."

Rufus glanced up a second time. "Can I do this before you dash my hope like a kid's popped balloon at a birthday party?"

Sam rolled his eyes.

Rufus returned to previously posted photos on the business page before coming across a different plane photograph that gave off "Welcome to the Company" vibes. The picture was a wide shot that included the tail numbers. "Oh! Found it. Let's see if this bad boy took a recent trip." Rufus opened a new browser page of a radar website and inputted the numbers. "This plane flew out of Maryland Wednesday—yesterday—and landed in New York a few minutes before nine in the morning."

He offered Sam the phone and pointed to the radar map covered in dozens of tiny planes. Underneath was a dropdown box of details relating to the tail number. "Before you ask, if Del got off the plane in the city, immediately caught a cab, and if the Morning Commute Gods were on his side, he definitely could have reached Shareed's hotel before she'd intended to meet you. But I want to stress he'd be cutting it extremely close."

For a silent moment, Sam studied the phone. "Or Lew could have done it for him."

"Yeah, I guess."

"Is there any way to see who was on the plane with him?"

Rufus shook his head. "No. They could have had Elvis onboard for all we know."

"So this doesn't tell us anything one way or another."

Rufus took his phone back. "It tells us when *some* of Conasauga's staff arrived, at least. It's better than nothing."

"I guess." Sam glanced around the taqueria, checked his phone, and frowned. "When is your appointment again?"

"Two o'clock."

"Let's get going. I don't want you to get bumped because we're late."

Rufus sighed loudly and got to his feet. He tossed their wrappers in the trash, bundled himself up against the cold, and pushed the door open. He said in a falsetto, while taking the stairs up to the sidewalk level, "And how does that make you feel, Rufus?" He turned and waited for Sam to join him before adding, "It makes me feel anxious and depressed, Dr. Donna, thanks for asking. I really can miss *one* appointment."

"Nice try."

Dr. Donna's office was on Thirty-Fifth Street—which was only a hop, skip, and jump away—except that she was on the *east* side of Manhattan. And even though the avenue blocks were twice the length of the streets, and at one point Rufus had had to take Sam's hand so he could speedwalk without losing his grumpier half, they'd managed to make it to his therapist's office with a handful of minutes to spare. The lobby was like every other modern office building in the city—lots of glass and reflective surfaces and ugly contemporary artwork. Rufus signed Sam in with the security desk before they took the elevator. At the seventh floor it was quiet and carpeted, with subdued gold lighting that felt far more welcoming than the downstairs had.

Rufus turned left and led the way down a long hall of private offices, coming to a stop at the very end outside of a frosted glass door with DONNA FITZGERALD, LP stenciled across it. He pointed to a small, padded bench beside a stand that held a fake orchid while saying, "You can wait here. Or, I guess you can come inside."

"I'll wait here." Sam cleared his throat. "Unless you want me to…."

"I don't know if you want to hear the kind of stuff I sometimes cry about." Rufus shrugged. He leaned close and kissed Sam. "I love you."

"I love you too." Sam dropped onto the bench. "But I'm going to wait here."

Rufus nodded. He tugged his beanie off and went inside without another word.

CHAPTER
FIFTEEN

Sam waited on the bench. The door to Dr. Donna's office was an effective sound barrier—or maybe the space on the other side was divided, and Rufus had passed into a second, inner room. Whatever the cause, he couldn't hear anything. Which was a good thing. He didn't even try to listen. He sat there, and the building generated its own low-grade percussion against the backdrop of the city's white noise: a series of opening and closing doors, echoing footsteps, a shrill of laughter ringing down the stairwell. Outside, the city was a muted roar.

For a while, he played back Cubs games. He'd been at game four for the clinch, 2015, the first postseason series at home that the Cubs had won. It had been against the Cardinals, which made it extra sweet. Then he flipped albums. Blind Willie McTell. The Lady. Muddy Waters. Hear that phone ringing, ringing, ringing. Another long-distance call.

When the door opened, he sat up straight and blinked. Rufus came out slowly, glancing in both directions before pulling the door shut.

Rufus tugged the black beanie over his shock of red hair. He smiled, and Sam knew him well enough these days to recognize the hurt hiding behind it, but also the authenticity in the way his mouth quirked to one side. "Ready?"

Sam nodded, and they headed out.

The walk back was worse. It was midafternoon, which in Manhattan, in winter, meant it was almost night. Clouds the color of raw linen tumbled overhead, and wind razored up the streets. The light was diffuse, yellow, tingeing everything with a sepia color. A cab almost clipped Sam at the second intersection. At the third, a woman was making her kids—a boy and a girl, neither of them old enough to be in school yet—dance while she rattled a cup full of change.

Inside the Javits was another world: sweat and wool, Italian suits, recirculated warmth, the buzz of fluorescents that Sam could feel in his teeth. They flashed their badges and headed down the escalator to the exhibition hall. Two men rode down behind them, both of them white guys, both of them in their thirties, both of them with the fleshy look of good drink and good food and not enough exercise.

"—seriously, her kids, man," one of them was saying. They both laughed.

"Thank God we took an Uber," the other one said.

Sam dug his thumb into a spot between his eyebrows. It was too bad, he thought, urban myths were just myths. The one about shoelaces on the escalator. The one about getting chewed up by the escalator's teeth.

The exhibition hall thrummed with its familiar energy. Attendees wandered from booth to booth, picking up complimentary keychains and flash drives and portfolio cases. Men—especially older, white men—came together in clumps and knots, ignoring the booths and the exhibits as they shook hands and laughed. A loud crack echoed through the hall, and Sam turned to see an older, balding man with a double chin laughing, while a girl who had to be a third his age tottered away on kitten heels. She was rubbing her backside and fighting to cover a look of outrage with a look of flirtatious amusement.

"Don't any of them carry guns?" Sam murmured. "There'd be a lot less ass-slapping if they knew they could get their dicks shot off."

Rufus pulled his lanyard over his head and passed it to Sam. "Hold this. I'll go kick him in the nuts until he's singing soprano."

Grinning, Sam caught Rufus's arm as they got off the escalator and tugged him away from the temptation.

A quick glance at the convention program gave them nothing; Evangeline Ridgeway wasn't scheduled on any panels for the rest of the afternoon. Neither was Colonel Bridges or Delmer Jolly or anyone from Conasauga. Lew hadn't appeared in any official presence in the convention schedule, and Sam figured whatever Lew's role, it had less to do with PowerPoints and more to do with beating people with socks full of pennies. He was willing to admit that might have been his imagination talking.

"Evangeline held on to the press release for a reason," Sam said when he and Rufus found a quiet spot against a wall. "And whatever the reason, she doesn't want to share. When we tried to talk to her, she blew smoke up our asses. I'd like to see what she has to say when we show it to her and ask about Shareed."

Rufus watched Sam carefully. "I agree. Del wasn't

taking the bait, but considering we found that in *her* room?" He shrugged, watched a gaggle of older men acting like college kids walk by, then added, "But if we're going to show our hand, we need to be careful. She's got a femme fatale thing going on."

Sam grunted. "Any ideas on where to find her?"

Pointing at a sign offering directions, Rufus said, "When she gave you the cold shoulder, she said that old geezer owed her a coffee. The center's café or bar might be a good bet, since she's not on any panels."

It turned out there was not one but two Starbucks inside the Javits. Because of course there were. Because it was fucking New York. The second-floor Starbucks was thronged by men and women in hipsterish gear: layers of sweaters and scarves and obnoxiously orange vests. One of them, with a ratty beard, was proclaiming loudly that he was only drinking the coffee because it would take too long to walk to an environmentally friendly, locally owned coffee shop, which he preferred to support because of the ethical concerns—

At which point, Sam stopped listening.

"I think we found the Habitat for Halibut crowd," he said, and then he pushed a long-haired guy in a distressed leather jacket out of his way and headed for the escalators.

The third-floor Starbucks was overrun by corporate types, but not the kind who were thronging the defense-contractor convention. For one thing, there were more women in this crowd. For another, although many of them were obviously proud of how expensive their clothes were, they were all dressed down compared to the defense executives—instead of suits and skirts, polos and khakis. A pair of generously endowed young women pranced past Sam and Rufus. They had been squeezed into tight pink t-shirts that said JUGHEADS, and the six-inch heels brought both of them to Sam's height. One of them was asking about supplier restrictions and bulk-order discounts.

"And here we have the franchise expo," Sam muttered. "Where the fuck is she?"

"Maybe she's moved on to day drinking," Rufus answered in a distracted manner. He was watching the women walk away. He put his hands to his chest and asked, "How'd they get into those shirts? It's like stuffing ten pounds of shit into a five-pound bag."

"Good Lord," Sam said and, of course, had to look again.

The Javits bar was on the ground floor. Like the rest of the convention center, it had a sleek, modern design: glass and stainless steel, pale woods and glowing polished-aggregate concrete. The crowd was smaller, although the hostess who passed them near the door had rings of sweat under her arms and slowed only long enough to wave them in, a gesture that Sam guessed meant "any open seat." The defense types seemed to dominate the day-drinking crowd. No sign of Evangeline.

Sam stepped aside to let a couple of older men in suits pass. "Motherfucker," he growled.

Rufus tapped Sam's arm and inclined his chin toward a high top at the midpoint between the bar and the booths against the wall. "There's that dumbass who was talking to Evangeline's chest this morning."

Sure enough, the young man whom Evangeline had called Anson was trying to strike up a conversation with an impeccably put-together blonde in a navy suit. Anson clearly had no idea that the woman was out of his league. He also didn't seem to be aware that women's ears were not co-located with their nipples. While Sam watched, the woman slid out of her seat, collected a small purse, said something with a smile that made Anson flinch and lean back in his chair, and clicked away on her heels. Anson made a delayed expression of outrage. Something about his hair and suit suggested, to Sam, anyway, Dartmouth. And lots of masturbation.

"God bless America," Sam said. "Come on. This asshole is going to get us Evangeline."

Rufus took the lead, winding his way through the tables and crowds. He came to a stop behind Anson, took a big step to the right, and then plopped his elbows on the tabletop. "Hey, bud." He glanced in the direction the blonde had gone and then gave Anson a nudge. "Win some, lose some, eh?"

"Excuse me?" Anson asked.

"She's out of your league," Rufus explained. "But hey, she's outta mine too. Don't get so worked up."

"Um, who are you?"

"Your new wingman," Rufus answered, giving Anson a second nudge. "Tip number one, stop looking at their boobs. It's too obvious. Go for the throat. That way you can do a quick flick up and down. It's less noticeable."

"Yeah, ok, whatever." Anson squirmed to the edge of his seat.

Sam shook his head and said, "No."

Anson sank back into his chair. He didn't exactly gulp, but he did get a little cheese-faced. He looked at Sam. Then he looked at Rufus. "I don't—I'm just having a drink, ok? I don't know what you want."

"Calm down, dude." Rufus smiled again. "I'm just trying to help you out. You know who I think would be perfect for you? Evangeline Ridgeway. D'you know her?"

Music came on the bar's speakers. It was something poppy, and Sam didn't recognize it. Anson flinched at the sudden rush of sound. Then he contorted himself, trying to look past Sam toward the bar's exit.

"Focus," Sam told him.

"Yeah, like, I know her." Anson seemed to think about

this and added, "Or whatever."

"Or whatever," Rufus repeated with a knowing grin. "How about you give her a call? A text? I bet you've got her business card, right? I bet that was the first thing you asked for."

"Uh, she airdropped me her contact info." Anson didn't exactly add *duh*, but it was clearly a struggle.

Rufus said to Sam, "Now he's just showing off." Looking at Anson again, Rufus said, "Go ahead and use that technology. Give her a call. Come *on*." He drew out "on" in a bro-ish attitude.

"I don't think—I think I'm going to go."

Sam made an interested noise and leaned forward, elbows on the back of the recently vacated chair.

This time, Anson did gulp. He pulled out his phone, glanced at Rufus—who was watching the screen—and tapped out a message. A moment later, his phone chimed.

"She, uh. She says she's finishing up a meeting. She'll be here, um, soon." Anson blinked rapidly. "You know."

"Great," Sam said. "In the meantime, you can tell us what you know about her and—"

The scream cut through the convention center's din. A woman's scream. Sam spun and sprinted toward the bar's exit.

He was too late. He wished he'd been later.

She hit twice: the up-escalator's rubber handrail, with the distinct crunch of breaking bones, and then the polished concrete floor on ground level. That sound was wetter, like a melon splitting. Sam stared into Evangeline's face. Her features were blank in death and distorted by the impact of her landing.

Then he looked up and saw Lew turning away from the third-floor railing.

CHAPTER
SIXTEEN

Rufus had been stuck between a rock and a hard place.

After having been caught red-handed at Shareed's crime scene by Erik—his ass still hurting from the chewing out that'd followed (metaphorically, of course)—Rufus wasn't in a rush to call the detective about a second dead body, hardly more than twenty-four hours later. But if he didn't, and word got out that a local CI was last spotted a few dozen feet from the dead and mangled body of a woman like Evangeline Ridgeway, who'd had an important job and impressive title and undoubtedly lots of connections and money.... Well, Rufus had seen far better people than himself get thrown under the bus in these kinds of situations. Calling Erik was, unfortunately, the safest option.

And after a bit of chest-thumping and rather inventive cussing, Erik had said he was on his way.

"We heard a scream," Rufus explained. He stood slouched against the glass wall of the concourse, arms crossed, staring at Erik's handsome face and thinking that he really could have been Ryan Gosling's younger brother. "Sam saw her fall from the escalator, hit the railing, then hit the floor." He added with a grimace, "The crunch echoed."

"And you saw somebody push her?" Erik asked Sam.

Sam shook his head.

"But you don't think this was suicide?"

Sam glanced at Rufus.

Rufus said, "According to my therapist, I have suicide ideation. But I can tell you this, I surely wouldn't chuck myself off an escalator if I were looking to get the job done."

"Right," Erik muttered.

"She's the one you asked about," Sam said. "What was the connection to Shareed Baker?"

"Baker called her from that hotel." Erik drew a deep breath. "What the fuck kind of trouble are you kicking up for me this time?"

Rufus held his hands up in defense. "Why do you always assume the worst of me? I've been taking in the sights with my beau and we came across this interesting convention. Give me a break."

"Bullshit."

"Bullshit, he says." Rufus dropped his hands. "Don't you think it's pretty suspish that Evangeline is dead a day after Shareed? And after you asked about her just last night?"

"All right." Erik stretched his back. "You know something about this. What the fuck is going on? All of it."

"If I knew what was going on, I surely fucking wouldn't be hanging out here for my health," Rufus said. "Shareed called Sam yesterday morning out of the blue. We had no idea who she was or how she got his number. She wanted to meet up and exchange some information, but instead she wound up dead. Now someone else is dead. I don't want Sam to be next."

"And you didn't think this was important to tell me when you called me out to see her dead body? A crime scene, by the way, that you two fucked to hell by trampling all over it."

"When you yell at me, Erik, I don't always want to phone a friend."

"You want to say something?" Erik asked Sam.

"I don't know what she had," Sam said. "But it's worth something to somebody. They killed her for it. And now they killed Evangeline."

"Why? Why her? What was her part in all of this?"

Rufus glanced at Sam before unbuttoning his jean jacket in order to produce the folded paper from Evangeline's hotel room. "We think Shareed was blackmailing Evangeline. I found this in her hotel room this morning. It's an old press release for something that never happened." He flipped it over. "And that's someone's banking info."

Snatching the paper, Erik made a disbelieving noise. He shook his head as he studied the page. Then he said, "This is mine now, understand? This is evidence. I don't want to know how you got into that hotel room. I don't want to know what else you've been doing. I want both of you to drop this. Right now." When Rufus opened his mouth, Erik spoke over him. "You don't want Sam to be next? Fine. Go play house and stay the fuck away from this. That's how you keep Sam from taking a tumble like this lady."

"It's not that simple," Sam said. "The people behind

this, they've already got me in their sights. Rufus too, I imagine."

"What is this? Some sort of Jack Ryan fucking TV special? Does one of you dumbfucks want to actually give me the whole story, or am I supposed to pick it up in between commercial breaks?"

"I wish Jack Ryan was involved," Rufus began. "John Krasinski got all bulked up for that show and he's pretty hot now." At the look on Erik's face, Rufus dropped the commentary. "We can't tell you everything that's going on, because we don't *know* everything that's going on. You name-dropped Evangeline and we traced her to here. Whatever's happening, it's multilayered and scary. Are you *sure* you can't tell us anything more about Shareed?"

Hands on hips, Erik studied them for what felt like a long moment. "She flew in Monday. Late. Came in on a plane from Atlanta. You already know where she was staying because you shat all over my crime scene. She called that Ridgeway woman. She called a hotel just around the block. She went there—we've got her on camera on the eighteenth floor." Erik blew out a breath. "Of course, the dumbfucks only put cameras in the elevator, so we don't know which room she went to."

Rufus made a face and glanced at Sam. "Eighteenth floor?" he repeated.

"What?" Erik asked.

"Just making sure," Sam said.

"Well, there you go. Nothing that screams conspiracy. She made some phone calls. She got some phone calls—"

"She got some phone calls?" Sam asked.

"Paranoia explains Cyber 44," Rufus mumbled.

Erik ignored that. "—she bought something to shoot up with. She went to a hotel. I could write it off as an OD with what I've got."

Rufus pointed discreetly to the escalators roped off with yellow crime scene tape. "Sure hope you don't write that off as an OD."

Erik flipped him the bird. "I've got work to do. Unless you've got something useful for me?"

Rufus shook his head and buttoned his jacket. "I got nada." He took Sam's hand and walked away from Erik, hugging the glass wall until they reached the front doors, where a uniformed officer let them exit without a parting glance. Once they'd put about a block of distance between them and the Javits, Rufus said, "Evangeline wasn't staying on the eighteenth floor."

"Nope," Sam said.

Rufus hunched his shoulders against the wind. "You think Erik could have been referring to Del's room?"

"Has to be. He was waiting in the lobby."

"If we could get in his room," Rufus started, "maybe we'd be able to prove he was full of shit about not knowing Shareed."

"He freaked out pretty good when you showed him that press release." Sam paused. "That could have had something to do with you accusing him of murder, I guess."

"Shareed OD'ing seems pretty unlikely now. At least, if she did, I think she might have had help from someone. Maybe not Del, but something about him definitely isn't kosher. Plus, I didn't mention it before, but he thought I was trying to cruise him. Gross."

The grin only lasted an instant. "What now?"

Rufus answered, "I think we should check out the eighteenth floor of the Savoy and see who might be home."

CHAPTER
SEVENTEEN

The Savoy-Hell's Kitchen was a different beast in the early evening. The same white-brick veneer, the same chrome trim, the same lobby with the same muted carpet squares and the same knockoff Scandinavian furniture, sure. But entirely different in ways that mattered.

Outside, darkness was settling over the city, but the Savoy-Hell's Kitchen's lobby was ablaze with light and sound. Men and women—but predominantly women—thronged the lobby. They were spilling out of the bar, most of them with drinks in hand, and they were laughing and talking at a migraine-inducing volume. They were uniformly dressed in what someone, somewhere, would have called business casual: lots of wool and corduroy and silk, lots of pastel blouses and paisley pashminas, lots of cutesy button-ups. One woman, in a violently striped blazer, was apparently demonstrating the stretchability of her trousers by extending one leg along the back of a sofa to the admiring noises of spectators.

"What in God's name is going on in this city?" Sam asked in an underbreath as he scowled a flabby-necked man in an ill-fitting polo out of his way.

Rufus shrugged. "Even I'm not sure sometimes."

The front desk clerk had changed since their visit that morning. The white boy with the locs was gone, and in his place was an older Asian woman, her thick, graying hair in a braid. She was staring into the middle distance. Maybe, like Sam, she was thinking New York City was ripe for another period of glacial expansion.

As Sam crossed to the bank of elevators, he considered her for a moment. "Does she look amenable to bribes?"

"Not even remotely," Rufus answered. He punched the Up button, and when the doors opened, he tugged Sam inside and hit 18. "It's a shame we don't have a gift basket," he said thoughtfully. "People always open their door for those chocolate and pecan turtles."

After that, they rode up in silence. The elevator stopped only once, on 11, where a nervous-looking woman laughed and apologized for hitting the wrong button. When it reached 18, the doors rattled open, and the smell of carpet cleaner and recirculated air rolled into the car.

Sam stepped out and checked the hall in both directions. At one end, a window looked out on the city at night. At the other, a painting—a vase full of flowers—hung on an otherwise blank hall. Sam counted six doors.

"Only six?" he asked.

"It must be one of the rich-people floors." Rufus sniffed the air. "Yup. Smells like money. Executive suites, I bet."

"Any guesses which one she went to?"

Rufus glanced in both directions as Sam had, then said, "If I had the money to stay here, I kind of feel like you're obligated to ask for a room with a view." He pointed toward the hall with the window.

"That leaves three."

Sam moved down the hallway. He stopped at the door to the room closest to the elevator and listened. Either the construction and materials were high enough quality to keep him from hearing anything, or the room was currently unoccupied. He moved to the next door, which was located on the opposite side of the hallway. He listened again. This time, the murmur of a television filtered out into the hallway. It sounded like a news channel, the voices steady and even. Behind him, Sam heard the elevator doors rattle shut as the car was called to another floor. He sent up a mental prayer that the woman with the stretchable pants didn't need to do a demonstration on the eighteenth floor.

The third door—1806—was on the same side of the hallway as the first. Sam listened. A man was talking. The voice had a low, snapping energy, but it didn't sound familiar. He'd heard Del Jolly speak twice now: at the Conasauga panel, and then at the hotel. Both times, Del had spoken in the varnished, self-assured tones of someone who believed money could smooth out any misunderstanding, and this didn't sound the same.

Sam retreated to the elevators. One of the cars was still going down. The other was stopped at the lobby. He took out his phone, did a web search for this hotel, and placed the call.

"Savoy-Hell's Kitchen," a woman answered. "This is Katrina, how may I help you?"

"Could you connect me with room 1806, please?"

"One moment, please."

Muzak picked up, and then immediately cut off as the phone began to ring. One, two, three—

"Yes, what?" It was the same snapping irritation Sam had heard through the door.

"Hello, Del?"

"Who?"

"I'm sorry, I'm trying to reach Del Jolly."

"Wrong number."

The receiver clattered against the cradle, and the call disconnected.

At Rufus's inquiring look, Sam shook his head. He considered the remaining rooms. Would Del Jolly want the room closest to the elevator? Or was he in the room with the television on? He flipped a coin in his head and pointed to the door closest to the elevator. "So, we knock?"

"I'm bold, but not that bold," Rufus answered. "Call again and ask for 1802."

Sam repeated his trick, if that's what you could call it, with the front desk. This time, the call rang until it bounced back to the front desk. Sam disconnected as Katrina started speaking again.

"Nobody's home," he said. "Or, at least, nobody's answering."

"More to my liking." Rufus tugged the DO NOT DISTURB sign off the doorknob of 1806 and held it up. "I can try to break in, if you're ready for that."

Sam nodded.

Rufus approached 1802 from an angle, careful to stay out of view of the peephole, in case someone *was* home and had simply been feeling uncommunicative. The door to the suite wasn't entirely flush with the frame—a small bit of space allowing for the deadbolt to be visible. Sticking the heavy-duty plastic hanger against the lock, Rufus gently wiggled it back and forth until the deadbolt clicked, which caused the keycard reader to flash green. He grabbed the knob and pushed the door open while looking toward Sam.

"That actually worked?" Sam murmured, catching the door on his shoulder as he stepped past Rufus. He stopped. The white hiss of the HVAC system met him; nothing else. Elbowing the door open the rest of the way, Sam took in the room.

Unlike a standard hotel room, the door opened onto a large living space with a seating area, a large television, and a wet bar. A single lamp gave enough light to see that the Savoy's Nordic design continued here with blond wood and chrome and glass. On the far side of the room, a wall of windows gave a view of the city that Del had undoubtedly paid a pretty penny for, the darkness shattered by the blaze of neon and sodium. A hall stretched off to the left, shadowy where the light from the lamp didn't reach.

Giving the door another nudge for Rufus to follow, Sam headed into the room. He drew the Beretta from his waistband and held it low against his thigh. The rush of circulating air seemed enormously loud, somehow, swallowing up everything else. His reflection moved with him in the glass.

The training came back, the way it always did. He found the light switch and cleared the hallway. Then an empty bedroom and a bathroom that looked like it hadn't been touched. Then a larger bedroom, a suitcase open on a stand. The door to the walk-in closet was open, and—

And instead of suits and dress shirts, uniforms hung in the closet. Army uniforms.

This wasn't Del Jolly's room.

A whiff of something foul met him as he approached the door to the attached bathroom, and a part of him already knew, even before he turned on the lights.

He was right about the blood on the tile, the streaks and swirls running down toward the shower drain. Right, too, about the smell you never forgot: a body violated, and shit, and piss.

But, then again, sometimes he was wrong.

Because it wasn't Del Jolly who had been shot twice in the chest and died in a luxury hotel in Hell's Kitchen. It was Colonel Leslie Bridges.

His face looked smaller in death, and the rictus made his little rat teeth even more prominent. He was still wearing the wool overcoat and the navy suit. A black driving glove—a little affectation, Sam guessed—had fallen out of his pocket and lay on the shower floor.

"Rufus," Sam called.

"Sam," Rufus answered back, his voice growing steadier in volume, like he was walking toward the en suite. "There're two glasses made up in the other room and liquor missing from the bar. Someone had a friend over for—holy shit what the *fuck*!" Rufus stood in the bathroom doorway, hands firmly in his jacket pockets, eyes wide with shock.

"Have you touched anything?" Sam asked.

"No," Rufus said with a vicious headshake. He pointed through his jean jacket, the gesture sort of looking like a kid trying to convince someone they had a gun in their pocket. "What'd you do?"

Sam shook his head. Then, returning the Beretta to the small of his back, he said in a low voice, "What the fuck?"

"Isn't that the colonel?"

"That's him."

"For Christ's sake," Rufus said on a shaky exhale. He tugged his hands free and was already pulling on his cheap winter gloves. He motioned Sam away from the body while stepping into the bathroom himself. "I could be naked in bed, eating leftover Chinese takeout off your perfectly sculpted butt cheeks, but instead I'm rummaging through the pants of a guy who's shit himself."

"Try not to—"

"Touch anything, yeah, yeah." Rufus crouched beside Bridges, his face twisted up in response to the smell. He carefully patted the dead man's trouser pockets before peeling back one side of his overcoat. Rufus studied the bloody chest wound for only a second before draping the coat back into place. He patted the outer pockets, and when something crinkled, reached inside. Retrieving a few folded and slightly crumpled sheets of paper, he shifted his weight onto one foot, reached out, and offered them to Sam.

Sam took them, angling them to catch the light. The formatting at the top was a blur at first, and then he processed it as the header of an email. He scanned the text and stopped and held out the page for Rufus's inspection, his thumb under the word STONEFISH.

CHAPTER
EIGHTEEN

The radiator was *ping*, *ping*, *ping*ing when Rufus and Sam stepped through the front door of the tiny tenement studio just after seven o'clock. Rufus held a pizza box in both hands—paid for with an IOU. He kicked the door shut, shoved the box onto the miniscule counter space, and let out a held breath. He dug his burner phone free, thumb hovering over the touchscreen for a long moment before he reluctantly inputted Erik's number.

The city hadn't been the free-for-all of Rufus's childhood for a long time. Back then, bad men could get away with unfathomable crimes simply due to the lack of surveillance or security footage for the law to fall back on. Nowadays, there were cameras everywhere. Not just at ATM machines or inside retail shops, but at traffic lights, on subway platforms, inside apartment lobbies, even elevators. And while Rufus was good at looking unimportant, was great even, at being forgettable, Erik hadn't been born yesterday. He'd been the one to mention the eighteenth floor, the elevator, the footage. And when Colonel Bridges's body would eventually be discovered by housekeeping, Erik would be checking the cameras again. He'd see his CI right there in the middle of it.

Rufus needed to establish his whereabouts with his handler before things got messy.

Messier, he thought, when Erik picked up.

Rufus wasted no time in admitting that they hadn't gone directly home to "play house," but had instead found a DB in the en suite bathroom of room 1802 at the Savoy, although he kept the email printouts found on the colonel's body to himself. Rufus had to practically yell over Erik's explosive bitching that he'd been out to lunch at Diabla around noon—ask the staff if they remember the redhead who asked for no ice and, like, three refills of Pepsi—he'd been at his scheduled therapy afterward—Sam was even signed in at the front desk—and then they'd been at the Javits when Evangeline had gone kaput. There was simply no possibility, based on the level of rigor seen in the body, that Rufus could be involved with the murder.

Rufus wasn't a killer, for Christ's sake.

He was just having some monumentally bad luck this week.

Maybe it was a full moon.

Or maybe Mercury was in retrograde. Isn't that what astrology girlies usually blamed for their shitty day?

After Rufus hung up, he tossed the cell onto the pizza box, but it slid off the cardboard and fell into the sink with an obnoxious clatter.

He left it there. "Come eat something."

"Someone shot him," Sam said. He pushed a hand through his hair. "Twice. What the fuck is that?"

Rufus cast his winter garments to the floor. He flipped open the lid on the box and removed a slice. He folded the pizza, took a big bite, then asked between chews, "How relevant is the argument the colonel had with Del in the hotel bar, you think?"

Sam didn't appear to have heard him. He rubbed his chin, expression distant, and then said again as though speaking to himself, "What the fuck *is* that? What does he *want*?"

Rufus had started to raise the pizza to his mouth again, but stopped. "He who? Del?"

"Del? No, Lew."

Rufus dropped the slice back into the box and wiped his hands on his jeans. "What the fuck's Lew got to do with the dead colonel?"

"What the fuck does he have to do with it? What does that mean? He's been up to his ass in this from the beginning, Rufus. She said his name—Shareed, I mean. And Stonefish, Went—do you want me to draw you a map?"

"We talked about this already. Before accusing Lew like we're in a game of Clue, you've got to look at the available evidence objectively."

Sam drew a deep breath. Then he shucked his coat and sat on the bed to undo his boots.

At Sam's non-answer, Rufus rolled his eyes. "The silent treatment. Cool."

"I think we could use some silence," Sam said. He scooted back along the mattress until his back was pressed against the wall, flattened the emails Rufus had taken from the colonel against his thigh, and bent over them like a man who was choosing to read instead of commit murder.

Rufus stood at the sink, his back to Sam. He finished the slice of mostly cold pizza. After, he retrieved his phone, got a drink from the tap to wash the wedge of crust down his throat, and took the box to the bed. He dropped it on the floor, motioned to it like Sam could help himself, then sat on the mattress. He held a hand out. "Can I read those too?"

Sam grunted and slid the pages he'd already read toward Rufus.

Rufus read the entirety of each printed email twice, from header to footer, because he didn't want to keep feeling ignorant about military whatchamacallits and thingamajigs. The back and forth between Del Jolly and Colonel Leslie Bridges, in his uneducated opinion, seemingly amounted to: Do me a big favor? Stonefish got a little fucked. Can you keep that on the DL so Conasauga keeps getting government contracts? Thanks, babe, I owe ya.

Rufus didn't need a college degree to recognize blackmail material. He understood now what Shareed had been doing in the elevator, what she'd been delivering to the eighteenth floor. Looking sideways, Rufus couldn't tell if Sam was still reading or pretending. So he just stated, "If the colonel knew about Conasauga's past fuckups, would that be enough reason to consider him a danger to the company's future? Enough of a danger to Del's success?"

"Maybe." Sam was staring off into space. "He said, 'We had a deal.'"

Rufus tapped the pages he held in one hand. "This."

"Yeah, of course, but—" He stopped again. "That's not how it sounded. He said—how did he say it? 'I did what you wanted.' That's not quite it. Del was practically begging. He didn't sound like a man who was about to kill someone."

His voice low, Rufus murmured, "People kill when

they're afraid, Sam."

Sam rubbed his thumb between his eyebrows. After what felt like a long time, he said, "He kills the colonel, but he leaves incriminating paperwork on the body. What's that about?"

"I don't know," Rufus said, doing his best to keep irritation from coloring his tone. "So Del's an idiot. Maybe he's not good at killing people and freaked out. Like a panic attack."

"He killed him in the shower. Two shots to the chest. That's not a panic attack, that's an execution."

Rufus set aside the papers and climbed to his feet. "We both know I'm an idiot, so explain to me why you don't believe, based on the content of those emails, that Del wouldn't have reason to kill the colonel."

"You're not an idiot. That's not what I meant." Sam pulled on his shirt the way he did sometimes when the sensory overload got to be too much, but his voice stayed level—or close enough. "What if it was Lew? What if it was someone else, I mean. Someone trying to make it look like Del did this. Isn't that at least a possibility?"

Rufus reluctantly leaned down to be eye level. "It's a possibility," he agreed. "It's just… I hesitate to believe *that* level of subterfuge is actually going on."

Music filtered into the apartment—AC/DC. And, right on cue, a moment later Pauly Paul began to sing. Badly.

"All right," Sam said. "It doesn't matter."

"It doesn't?"

"Whether Lew did this or—or Del, either way, this is proof that Stonefish was a cover-up. You saw the emails; Del needed Stonefish to go away, and the colonel made it go away. And that means somebody, somewhere, knows what really happened to Went."

Rufus was quiet as he slowly drew himself back up

to his full, albeit lanky, height. He considered how to say this—because if you didn't know the intimate ins and outs of depression, if you didn't know that crippling, debilitating sense of hopelessness, the ideation that was far stronger than the fear of death, of the unknown, that made a bullet or a rooftop feel like the only answer, the only way out, the truth could sound... cruel. But Rufus decided, even if it hurt beyond measure to hear, Sam would know it came from a place of real understanding.

"Sometimes... people just want to die. Sometimes life eats at you until you've had enough—until you can't do it anymore. Sometimes, there's no conspiracy."

Sam nodded. "But at least I'd know."

CHAPTER
NINETEEN

Sleep came slowly for Sam, and when he dreamed, it was in broken images—the Savoy, the Javits, the dark tunnel of Manhattan. Through all the dreams, an undertow dragged on him, and in the dream, he knew it was like the gravity that had made Evangeline Ridgeway's fall true as a plumb line. When he woke, the apartment was gray with the morning, and the thing pulling on him was Rufus, who had turned until the bedding was caught around him, winching Sam along with it.

He showered. A fresh tee. Clean jeans. His ruck, when he was done, was ready to go again.

Go where, he thought.

The thing pulling on him. Like gravity.

He read the news on his phone as Rufus stirred, peed, leaned in the doorway, scratching under one arm. It was time to be an adult about the night before, about his… reaction.

But then he saw the next headline and said, "Rufus."

SAVOY SLAYING it said, with all the *New York Post*'s usual class. And then, in case you didn't get it, HOTEL HOMICIDE was printed immediately underneath.

"Police have not released the victim's identity," Sam read as he angled the phone for Rufus to see, "but sources close to the investigation say that the victim was a government employee, possibly associated with the U.S. military. Police have yet to comment on the status of the investigation."

"Sonofabitch," Rufus grumbled. He hastily dug through his clothes on the floor, stopping to smell a few shirts. "The *Post* moves fast." He yanked a black thermal over his head. "At least we weren't mentioned."

"Maybe we'll get lucky and they'll see whoever came out of that room."

"Like Del?" Rufus tugged on black skinny jeans, buttoned them, and added, "I think we should find him, get it straight from the horse's mouth, and then toss him to the wolves before Erik decides his CI is too hot to keep on payroll. That article didn't say anything about a suspect yet, did it?" He went digging for a t-shirt.

"Not yet," Sam said sourly. "Any ideas on *how* to track down Del? Somebody with that much money is probably hiding behind an army of lawyers, and I doubt he gave the Savoy his forwarding address."

Rufus had retrieved a t-shirt that said CRIME PAYS in bold letters. "I think better when I've been fed, you know."

There was something to be said for consistency. In spite of himself, Sam smiled. "BlueMoon?"

Rufus met Sam's look with a toothy grin of his own. "Baby, it's like you love me."

As far as Sam was concerned, there wasn't a lot to like about New York. The city was too loud, too busy, and simply too *much*. Like the girl Sam had seen on one of his rare subway rides—she'd been drooping, lurching every time the train moved, and all of a sudden, she'd puffed out her cheeks like a blowfish and stayed that way the rest of the ride. (It had been the A, of course.) At the next stop, she'd stumbled off so she could spit out approximately a gallon of vomit in the closest trash can. There was the guy in the park next to Rufus's building who dressed up like a rat and climbed around on the benches. One time, they'd been waiting in line in a deli, and these two old ladies had been going at each other, screaming louder and louder until one of them stabbed the other with a plastic fork. And then, fuck of all fucks, they'd both burst out laughing.

So, that was New York, for Sam.

But the city did have one thing: it had BlueMoon.

And, of course, it had Rufus.

The diner wasn't much to look at. The glass door was covered in stickers, lots of them for bands Sam had never heard of, although he guessed Rufus probably had. Inside, the aesthetic was vintage American, meaning: old as shit, but well kept. It smelled like good coffee and a seasoned griddle, and the menus had that film on them that made them feel perpetually greasy, and the short-order cook rang a bell every time a plate was up. But somehow, it never felt like too much. That might have been because of the pancakes.

They took their usual spot, and it wasn't until Sam was in the booth that he realized he'd thought of it as *their* spot. He wasn't sure when it had stopped being *Rufus's* spot.

"On my way, Freckles," Maddie called from the register.

Sure enough, she came over with coffees and menus—not that they needed the menus at this point. They ordered: the BlueMoon's version of a Grand Slam for Sam, and for Rufus, pancakes. Some days, Maddie lingered to chat, but today the arrival of more customers meant she left them with nothing but a quick pat on the shoulder for each man.

"I was thinking…" Sam said. "What's to say Del hasn't skipped town already?"

"Wouldn't it look suspicious?" Rufus tore open a sugar packet and poured the contents into his palm. "Disappearing during the middle of that Big Dick Energy convention would have to look weird to someone, I'd think."

"Sure. But I don't know if that would stop him."

Rufus dumped the sugar into his mouth, wiped his hands on his jeans, then awkwardly shrugged out of his jacket. He yanked free the convention schedule that was beginning to look like it'd been run over by a truck or possibly chewed on by a dog. Thumbing through the pages, Rufus said, "Del's supposed to be at the Javits today. He's a guest speaker on an afternoon panel."

"So, he might be there."

"Even if he's not, we should listen to what folks might be saying about him being MIA."

"Or arrested," Sam said. "But I doubt we'll be that lucky."

At that, Rufus picked up the saltshaker, poured some into his hand, then tossed it over his shoulder. "I read that's supposed to be lucky. Or was it about warding off evil…? Something superstitious like that."

Sam wasn't sure how well it was working, considering Maddie made Rufus sweep it up about five seconds later.

Their food came, and they ate—not exactly in silence, but in the quiet of people with no particular need to say anything. What Sam didn't finish (the pancakes), Rufus did. The day was growing steadily brighter, the street on the other side of the plate-glass windows taking on depth, but it wasn't by any means a *bright* day. The clouds were low and gray, and the light was the same color as if it were coming through a sheet of newspaper.

When they'd finished—meaning the plates had been scraped clean—Sam counted out cash for the check. "I want to get over there early and see if anyone's talking about the colonel. That all right?"

"I have so many other pressing engagements on my social calendar," Rufus was saying as he began bundling himself back into his winter gear. "But for you? I'm willing to clear my schedule."

"That sounds like the pancakes talking."

"I think I ate too many," Rufus agreed as he followed Sam toward the door.

Sam was proud of himself for not even saying, *Huh*.

They made their way toward the Javits. The wind whistled in Sam's ears, loud enough almost to drown out the incessant sounds of traffic, and granules of snow—closer to ice—spun around him, stinging his cheeks and ears. Sam tried to lose himself in his thoughts, but the noise and the nonstop movement around him made it impossible. A woman zipped past him. A man stopped unexpectedly to stare at his phone. Cars sped up, engines rumbling. At the next intersection, the light changed. Cars braked and queued. That was why, when the black town car slowed at the curb, it registered as only one more intrusion among many.

Then the rear window buzzed down, and a man said, "Mr. Auden?"

He was white, somewhere between thirty and forty, and from what Sam could see, built stockily. He wore his hair buzzed, and he leaned toward jug-eared, and it looked like he'd spent a lot of his life in the sun. Sam didn't know him, but he knew the type.

"I'd like to talk to you," the man continued. "And your friend. If you have a minute?"

"We have no minutes, actually," Rufus answered while leaning around Sam. He gave Sam's arm a tug and said, quieter, "Come on."

The attack came from behind.

The first blow landed low on Sam's back, almost at the base of the spine. It was more shock than pain, and the force of it sent him staggering forward a step. Then a hand caught him by the hair and smashed his face into the roof of the town car.

CHAPTER
TWENTY

Blood spurted from Sam's nose, or maybe it was his mouth, and Rufus shouted, "Holy shit!" before instinctively dodging to the right—out of the line of fire. He overstepped, lost his balance, grabbed for the pole of a NO PARKING sign, slipped on a patch of ice, then crashed into a pile of black trash bags sitting curbside for pick-up. Pain shot from his tailbone and ricocheted up his spine. Rufus heard the flurry of creative cusses begin pouring from his mouth like he had switched onto automatic pilot, but when he looked up in time to see Sam go at his attacker, only to take a gut punch and double over, the words dried up in his throat like a desert oasis that turned out to be a mirage.

When the back door of the car opened, Rufus looked on either side of himself, grabbed the closest thing he could find among the trash, and scrambled to his feet. He flung himself onto the car door, slammed it shut before the stranger had a chance to climb out, and breathlessly, Rufus said, "Hey, you Dumbo-eared motherfucker, do you have any idea the kinda nutcases who live in this city? You can't just stop to chat with any rando on the street. You might come across an antichrist with a hit list." He raised an unopened Coke can in one hand. "Any fucking idea what this is? It's a *homemade bomb*. You wanna try me?"

The man blinked once.

Rufus could see the mental gears turning.

Then the man gave the door a second shove open.

"Hey! No—you stupid—" Rufus pushed back on it, the soles of his Cons scraping the salty cement as he lost ground. He gave the Coke can a quick shake, put his hand through the open window, and pulled the tab. Soda sprayed out in a huge gush, coating the expensive interior and jarhead-looking stranger. The man fell back onto the leather seats, loudly protesting and wiping his face.

At that moment, Sam staggered back against the car. It rocked under his weight, and Sam dipped with it. He tucked his chin and caught the next punch on his shoulder. Blood coated his mouth, but he seemed to have recovered from the surprise—no sooner had the punch landed than Sam was already throwing a cross. A painful, fleshy cracking noise followed, and Rufus thought he'd just heard somebody's nose break.

Rufus wheeled back several steps, avoiding a misplaced punch to the face. The second man, who'd been on Sam, was now actively scrambling away. Red hair, Dr. Robotnik mustache—it was fucking *Chad* of the bodega coke sales. Seeing an opportunity, Rufus mirrored Chad's movements, got a hand into his pants pocket, and yanked free a wallet just as Jarhead was shouting and Chad cut his losses. He dodged around the front bumper of the car, dove into the passenger seat, and the driver peeled away from the side of the road.

Sam took a few unsteady steps after them. Then he stopped, hands on knees. He was shaking. One hand came up, as though checking the blood around his mouth, and he winced when his fingers brushed his nose.

"Shit," he said.

Rufus crouched before Sam to get a better look at his face. He frowned at the sight of red puffy skin and dripping blood, then gave the wallet a little wave. "Pay day."

CHAPTER
TWENTY-ONE

"God damn it," Sam said as Rufus dabbed at his face again with the wet paper towel. He tried to pull back, but the redhead had a surprisingly strong grip when he put his mind to something. As Rufus moved in for the kill again, Sam settled for asking, "Tell me again why we couldn't have gone back to your place to do this? Not that I don't have a special place in my heart for the men's room at the Javits."

In all fairness, it actually wasn't all that bad. It was clean—ish—and the smell of Sam's own blood was strong enough to cover any other odors that might have bothered him. More importantly, it was surprisingly empty, but then, they'd picked one of the facilities away from most of the foot traffic. The looks they'd gotten on their walk, as people gaped at Sam's possibly broken nose and bloodstained face and clothes, had almost been worth it.

"You're being a huge baby," Rufus muttered as he worked, carefully rubbing at the crusted blood under Sam's nose. "Can you breathe? Is it broken?"

"No clue." But when Sam checked himself in the mirror, he said, "I don't think so." Rufus had done a good job—the blood was gone except for a few dark drops on his clothes. His nose was puffier than usual, but it didn't look crooked or bent, and when Sam probed gently, it felt sore instead of painful. He turned back to Rufus and gave him another once-over; Rufus had already insisted that he was fine, but—"How's your ass?"

"Wanna kiss it?"

"Playtime's later." But Sam brushed his fingertips along Rufus's hairline and kissed him. "You're sure you're ok?"

"Yeah, I'm fine. I'm not the one who went face-first into a car." Rufus tossed the paper towels. "I'm glad you're tougher than old boots."

"Is that an expression?"

"Sure it is." Rufus shrugged and smiled—a little less cockier than usual, but given the situation, that was expected. He cleared his throat before producing the wallet he'd lifted. "Here you go. Keep whatever cash he's got. I probably owe you."

"Maybe it's more like a joint checking account." But Sam took the wallet and opened it.

Two hundred and forty-three dollars. An unmarked keycard—not the cheap, thin kind that hotels gave out, but a solid piece of plastic that was meant to last for a long time. A business, maybe. An unopened scalpel blade in sterile packaging. A bump of coke. A crumpled receipt for McAlister's Steak House. And a driver's license for Chad Deangelis. The photo on the ID matched the man Sam had fought on the street, down to the ridiculous mustache, and as far as he could tell, the license was real.

"Call Erik?"

Rufus was making a face now. "Everyone I'm working with thought Chad was just some lowlife coke dealer… but he's gotta be connected. Maybe he's got a lawyer on retainer. Because two days after I put the NYPD on his ass he shows up outta nowhere in a swanky car? He should be booked downtown. I think it might be in our best interest to first look for what's connecting him to all this."

Sam nodded. He folded the cash into his wallet, handed the license to Rufus, and said, "Assuming that's legit, I guess he wasn't worried about anybody knowing who he was."

"Looks real to me," Rufus agreed, flipping the New York ID back and forth to study either side. "It's got the raised signature and funky holograph. Those are tough to make on the street. Can't believe his name really *is* Chad."

"Chad likes rib eyes. And he's not smart enough to buy his wine by the bottle—how many glasses did this asshole have?" Sam held out the receipt. "Do you know this place?"

"That many zeroes isn't my lifestyle. But the address isn't far from here—somewhere in Chelsea."

"Ok. So, town car, expensive dinner, keycard. But on the other hand, a scalpel blade, a bump of coke, and more cash than most people carry. Not to mention the fact that they planned that shit show." Sam touched his nose gingerly again. "The guy I saw in the car looked like he could have been military, but Chad—" He flicked the license. "—I don't know. And if they're with Lew, why are they riding around in a fucking town car and carrying a New York license?"

"Someone must have seen us hanging around here," Rufus said. "I bet they were waiting, hoping we'd come back today." He shoved the ID into his jacket pocket before putting his hands on his hips. "These asshats *could* be working for Del, right? I guess if that one guy is military, the situation does lean more in Lew's favor, but Chad being a local? That must be important."

"Right." Sam glanced at his watch. "We could check out the steakhouse. Or run down the address on the license. But I don't want to miss Del if he's here. I guess Chad's going to have to wait."

The rest of the morning and early afternoon they spent roaming the convention, on the hunt for any news about Del Jolly, Conasauga, or the colonel. It wasn't like they had to find a way to bring the topics up—the majority of people at the convention, it turned out, were people who loved to hear themselves talk, and everybody was talking about the colonel's death and Evangeline's possible suicide. It was simply a matter of moving through the convention hall, stopping to listen where conversational knots had formed, and then moving on again when the time was right.

The problem, though, was that even though everyone was talking about the colonel, nobody was saying anything useful. Sam heard the same information repeated over and over again, the bare details of the case embroidered with rumor and suspicion. That it had something to do with organized crime. That it had something to do with drugs.

What he didn't hear—not even once—was a word about Stonefish. And he wondered if whoever had killed the colonel was pissed that those incriminating emails had never made it to the authorities. When Lew got pissed, he got quiet, but you could see it in the way he clenched his jaw.

There wasn't any sign of Lew, though—pissed or otherwise. And no sign of Del, either, although Sam didn't think that was too surprising—if Del *had* stuck around, he might not want to poke his head out until he absolutely had to. With Evangeline dead, and now the colonel, everybody around him was dropping like flies.

When Sam tracked Rufus down in the convention center's bar shortly before Del's panel was scheduled to begin, the first thing he said was something else he'd noticed.

"Looks smaller today, doesn't it?"

"I was thinking the same thing," Rufus answered. He'd taken up residence in the back of the bar, standing at one of the high-top tables hardly big enough for two people to set their cocktails on. "I didn't want to be dramatic, but maybe these deaths really spooked the Suits."

"Yeah, I think normally these things are mostly an excuse for a bunch of middle-aged men to talk over each other and carry their Viagra prescriptions around. Somebody takes a dive in the middle of that? And somebody else gets shot in a hotel room? Talk about boner killers." He scanned the crowd once more, but he still didn't see Lew or Del. "Any luck?"

"With my boner? It works just—oh, you mean Del. No, I didn't see him."

"Same here. No sign of Lew or Del yet. Should we try the panel?"

Rufus gave the tabletop a quick drum with his fingers. "At this rate, I'd say it'd be pretty ballsy if Del was in attendance. But even if he's not, the excuse for his absence might tell us something." He took a step back while asking, "That's supposed to start in a few minutes, right?"

"Yep," Sam said. "Let's see what's going on."

When they got to the room where the panel was going to be held, Sam was unsurprised—if annoyed—to see that it was already full. People packed the spaces along the walls. One enterprising man was sitting on his briefcase. More bodies jammed the doorway, and the crowd spilled out into the hall. Sam returned the angry looks and mutters with hard looks of his own as he forced a path through the audience. It was actually easier that way, as a matter of fact—it gave him something else to think about.

They ended up near the front of the seats, pressed up against the wall, less than two yards from the tables where the panelists would be. A woman was already seated— Indian, Sam thought, with her dark hair cut short and in a suit that managed to look both understated and expensive. Then the crowd began to buzz. Men and women moved aside to clear a path, and a moment later, Del entered the room. He was followed a moment later by a second man— white, fortyish, with the kind of glasses that would have gotten him punched in elementary school—who was trying to read as he walked, his nose buried in a thick packet.

Another woman appeared to be the moderator, and she got the panel started. Each of the panelists presented something involving slides that showed pictures of military equipment, charts, and big numbers. None of it, as far as Sam could tell, had anything to do with Stonefish—Del's presentation had to do with some sort of data analysis software. All three presenters, in turn, seemed to veer between the highly technical and the grossly commercial— the subtext, when it *was* subtext—seemed to be simply: *buy from me.*

After about fifteen minutes of it, Sam found his mind wandering. He scanned the crowd. By this point, he was beginning to recognize faces that he'd seen at the convention, but no one he'd flagged as memorable or important. They all seemed to have varying degrees of interest in the presentations—the man on his briefcase was about to fall asleep, his head nodding as he inched closer to slipping off his impromptu seat.

Where was Lew?

There were lots of reasonable explanations for why Lew might not be at the panel—chief among them, the possibility that Lew had killed Colonel Bridges and framed Del for it. But if Rufus was right, and if Sam was looking for patterns that weren't there, then why wasn't Lew here? Maybe it was as simple as Lew no longer had a reason to attend the convention with the colonel dead. But that didn't seem to track; if anything, Lew's attendance should have been more important. And no matter what Rufus said, Sam hadn't imagined Lew's presence at the Conasauga panel on Wednesday—and if it had been so important then, where was he now?

He was so caught up in theories that, before he knew it, the panel was over. Most of the crowd dispersed, some of them clearly disappointed that Del hadn't confessed to murder, otherwise implicated himself, or had the decency to show up covered in blood. A few men and women lingered, though, clearly hoping to talk one-on-one. When it became clear that they wouldn't be able to catch Del alone, Sam nudged Rufus toward the hall.

"He's got to come out of there sometime," Sam said. "Let's see if we can get him alone somewhere."

Rufus pointed discreetly in one direction, saying, "There's a bathroom back that way. And over there is a corner that used to have a phone bank. If all else fails, we can bring him upstairs where the Halibut guys are."

Seconds turned into minutes. Convention-goers hurried past them. Voices echoed from the high ceiling, so many people talking at once that it all became an ebbing, swelling roar.

And then Del appeared, glancing blankly from side to side like a man crossing the street on autopilot, one hand checking that his shirt was tucked in. His gaze swept over them without seeming to take them in, and he turned and set off toward the front of the convention center.

Sam went after him, Rufus at his side. The bathrooms Rufus had indicated were ahead of them. Sam thought the easiest thing to do might be to take Del's arm—gently—and guide him toward the door. Most people, if you tried that, were so taken aback that they went along with you simply because they hadn't figured out what else they were supposed to do.

As Sam picked up his pace, closing on Del's flank, someone stepped into his path. Sam tried to jink past him, but the man moved with him, holding up a hand. At first, Sam registered it as a warning—STOP—but then the man said, "Hey!" and he realized it was a greeting.

Sam sidestepped again, and the man moved with him. He brought his attention to bear on the man, which meant losing track of Del for precious seconds.

The hair. The suit. The way this guy couldn't help but try to stare down the blouse of a woman passing him. Then his eyes came back to Sam, and he said, "God, I'm so glad I ran into you."

"Move, Anson," Sam said.

"I've been freaking out—"

"Move!" Sam didn't wait for an answer; he shoved Anson out of his way and started forward at a jog. Del was less than a hundred yards ahead, but that was significantly farther than he'd been a few moments before, and, worse, he'd already passed the bathrooms Sam had intended to use.

"It's just—" Anson sounded out of breath as he came after Sam. "—ever since, you know, Evangeline, I've been thinking."

"Rufus," Sam growled as he hurried after Del.

"Hey, buddy," Rufus said, already in the process of cutting Anson off from Sam's path. He flicked the other man's nose, held up a cell phone, and asked, "This yours?" And when Anson automatically reached for his pocket, Rufus drew his arm back and chucked it down the hall like he was trying out for the Yankees. "Go fetch."

Anson's outraged shout followed Sam as he broke into a run.

Ahead of him, Del was almost to the exit. The older man was still doing those nervous, side-to-side looks, but Sam got the impression they were instinct more than anything else—Del moved like a man who was nearly blind with his own panic. Sam's stride ate up the distance between them steadily. A hundred yards dropped to eighty. Then to sixty.

He was thirty yards back when Del shoved open the door and stepped outside.

It took five seconds, maybe six, for Sam to follow.

The clouds had thinned. Sunlight made him squint. The smell of exhaust rose to meet him, circulating on a draft of cold air.

At the curb, two men had their hands on Del Jolly's arms. As Sam watched, they shoved him into the back seat. One dove in after him, while the other hurried around to the driver's seat.

"Hey!" Sam shouted. He sprinted toward the car. "Stop!"

They peeled away from the curb, and at the next intersection, they turned and were gone.

CHAPTER
TWENTY-TWO

Rufus thought he'd been right behind Sam—it'd only taken seconds to relieve Anson of his phone and send it flying—but Sam had picked up speed between the bathrooms and the front lobby, and if it wasn't for his height and that stride Rufus had come to know so well, Rufus would have lost him in the ebb and flow of the Javits crowd.

Racing out the front doors, Rufus found Sam standing at the edge of the salt-crusted sidewalk, staring at the road ahead. "Hey!" Rufus skidded to a stop at his side, a cloud of white air puffing out on his exhale. "Where'd he go?"

Sam gestured toward the street. "Someone grabbed him." And then he shouted, "Fuck!"

"Someone grabbed—what, like something out of an old gangster flick? What'd they look like?"

People were starting to stare. Sam turned away from the street and lowered his voice. "I don't know. Two guys. White. It wasn't Chad and his friend. By the time I was out here, they had Del and were putting him in the car—a dark sedan."

Rufus made a *tsk* sound. He echoed Sam's "fuck" under his breath before sliding his plastic-frame sunglasses on. "Seems like someone wants to talk to Del as badly as we do."

"Or wants him *not* to talk. Let's get out of here."

Rufus was digging out the driver's license from his pocket as he followed Sam. "What about Chad? He's got an address on West 122nd Street. That's up in Harlem. We can knock and see if he's home."

Sam plucked at his shirt—even in the cold, he looked flushed from running. "I guess we're going to Harlem."

The Thirty-Fourth Street station was always a bit of a shitshow. The disorganized chaos from Penn Station had a tendency to bleed onto the subway platforms, leaving it the ideal hunting ground for pickpockets, rapists, and murderers alike—all depending on the time of day. This generally caused an uptick in police presence, which meant that Rufus couldn't easily jump the turnstiles unless there was a train already closing its doors and he was certain he could slide in just in the nick of time. But he was unwilling to take that chance when Sam was with him nowadays, not because Sam was incapable of a little fare evasion, but it was easier to do the petty theft stuff on his own, when Rufus wasn't responsible for someone else.

They'd swiped Metro cards under the watchful eye of a few beat cops wearing heavy jackets and NYPD winter beanies, caught the uptown A—one of the old R46 cars resembling a tin can—and rode it to 125th Street.

The neighborhood that had grown around 125th Street, known as the Main Street of Harlem, was rich in history, having once been a beacon for migrating Black families looking for higher wages and more equality than what was available to them in the deep south. This community had birthed the Harlem Renaissance—an explosive movement that explored Black music, art, literature, and politics after the first World War, forever changing the cultural landscape of America. But by the Great Depression, Harlem suffered from debilitating unemployment, housing discrimination, poor public services, and lack of educational opportunities more than any other neighborhood in New York City. The streets today were lined with historic landmarks, walkup tenements, and hundred-year-old brownstones, all reminders of the lives once lived here.

Chad Deangelis lived at 326 West 122nd Street, off the corner of Frederick Douglass Boulevard, in a five-story walkup of red brick and painted green trim. The front steps were salted, trash bins were all lined up against the building's façade, and the vestibule that was visible through the glass front door was clean.

Rufus checked the driver's license again. "2D. He's probably in the back. Want me to buzz him?"

"Let's see if he's home."

Rufus put his thumb on the button for 2D and leaned into it, letting it ring long enough to be so obnoxious that anyone at home would be hard-pressed to not respond. He let up, counted to five, then tried again. But when the second ring went unanswered, Rufus asked, "May I impress you with my breaking and entering skills?"

"Always."

Rufus pressed a few of the other buttons, and said, when 3A answered, "Amazon."

The front door buzzed open.

Rufus stepped inside. Held the door for Sam with one hand while giving 2D's wall mailbox a quick tap—a reminder that this was all real. He pushed through the inner vestibule door and onto a hallway. Chad's apartment was the first door on the second floor, and the doorknob looked old—like the landlord hadn't had a reason to replace it in a long time. Chad had probably lived there for a while, Rufus decided, otherwise a new tenant would ask for an up-to-date one. Motioning Sam to stand behind him and block his body from view, Rufus retrieved a pick from his jacket and went to work on the lock.

It only took a few seconds.

Rufus loved lazy security.

The door popped open and Rufus stepped aside while saying, "Age before beauty."

"Jesus, Rufus," Sam said as he stepped inside. But it sounded like he was smiling.

Rufus closed the door behind them and took a look around. The apartment was a spacious one-bedroom, ideal for someone living alone, which was the vibe for sure. Wasn't there a stereotype about straight men's bachelor pads? Something like mismatching bedsheets, no art or photos on the walls, and lots of sports memorabilia. Minus the sports, because it'd never been a big thing for Rufus— beyond booing the Red Sox because it was a matter of pride—he was uncomfortably aware of how similar his own apartment was to Chad's.

"Am I a straight bachelor?" Rufus asked, mostly to himself, as he crept through the railroad style kitchen and into the living room.

"How to tell you?" Sam mused.

"I wasn't talking to you," Rufus said over his shoulder. He stopped in the middle of the room. A leather couch, glass-top desk, ergonomic chair—gotta get that lumbar support—a squat bookshelf populated mostly by titles on economics and alpha male self-help guides, a bike shoved into the far corner that was probably never ridden, and an impressive television and entertainment setup. "Look at the size of this fucking screen," Rufus said with a low whistle.

"Look at the size of this apartment," Sam said drily. "His toilet's not in his kitchen."

"It's called multitasking, Sam."

"Back to your 'straight bachelor' comment."

Rufus rolled his eyes. "Are we here to be nosey or are we here to discuss my interior decorating skills?"

This time, the tone was *definitely* dry. "It's called multitasking."

"Oh my God, you've been hanging around me way too much." Rufus went to the bookshelf and began pulling at spines, checking for anything that might have been tucked behind the books.

Sam, meanwhile, moved into the bedroom. The sounds of a search drifted out to where Rufus was still working— the thud of the mattress falling back into place, the scrape of drawers that had swollen tight in the humidity, bifold doors rattling open.

"You're like a bull in a china shop," Rufus called, before stopping at a three-ring binder on one of the lower shelves. Half expecting a collection of baseball cards, he yanked it free and flipped through several pages before adding, "I think I found Chad's taxes or something."

Sam appeared in the doorway a moment later. "I want the little fucker to know somebody was here." His gaze fell on the binder. "No shit. Really?"

Rufus shrugged and then said, "It looks like expense reports, maybe?"

"What the fuck is he expensing?"

"Lots of meals. There's some bridge and tunnel tolls… airfare…." Rufus's voice trailed off for a minute before he looked toward Sam and clarified, "LaGuardia to Atlanta. He did that a few times. And there's some car rentals here too."

"You're kidding." But Sam's voice didn't sound like he thought it was a joke. "Benning is two hours from Atlanta. That's where he'd fly if…."

Rufus got down on one knee, set the open binder on the floor, and started taking pictures of each page with his phone. "Each of these reports is being expensed to the same company," he said. "Civic Catalyst."

CHAPTER
TWENTY-THREE

The bodega's name was mostly gone, the yellow awning bleached by the sun until it was closer to the color of heavy cream, and where the security gates were pulled shut at night, tears of rust stained the concrete. Inside, it smelled like coffee and cardboard and food under a heat lamp. The linoleum, where it was visible in the narrow aisles, was blue-and-white checkerboard, scuffed and stained from decades of traffic. One of the coolers was making an ominous grinding sound.

"No," Sam said to Rufus's offer of Takis, and went back to his phone.

Rufus had needed snacks.

Civic Catalyst had a minimalist website; it advertised

itself as one of the most effective lobbying firms in Washington (they didn't bother to add D.C. since, you know, you weren't their clientele if you didn't know that). Among their services, they offered strategic counsel, advocacy, intelligence gathering, policy analysis, and issue tracking. They even offered something called message creation, and whatever the fuck that was, it gave Sam the heebie-jeebies. The About Us page had a brief description of the firm's history—going all the way back to the Clinton era—and it included a picture of happy white people who looked like they spent a lot of time indoors. Sam didn't recognize any of the faces. Nobody named Chad was listed anywhere on the site, as far as he could tell.

"Anybody look familiar?" he asked, displaying the photo to Rufus.

Rufus crunched loudly on Takis while leaning over the phone's screen. "Nuh-uh. I mean, everyone at the Javits started bleeding together after a while, but I don't think we saw these guys."

Sam grunted and went back to research. Since the website was a dead end, he searched again for Civic Catalyst, but this time he added Conasauga.

The first result was for a site called OpenSecrets. It appeared to be dedicated to exposing the money behind politics—and behind politicians. The link took Sam to a page for an overview of Civic Catalyst. If this site was to be believed, Civic Catalyst had been hired by 127 clients the year before, for a total amount of $13,060,000. In one year. They had twenty-three full-time lobbyists. And when Sam scrolled down, he saw a list of clients that was sortable. When he sorted by the amount each company had paid, Conasauga was at the top. They'd paid Civic Catalyst almost half of their total annual amount—a little over six million dollars.

"Jesus Christ," Sam said.

"Jesus H. Christ," Rufus said almost at the same time. "Del's company must have a huge piggy bank—there's two commas in that number." He wiped his fingers clean on his jean leg before reaching over Sam's shoulder to scroll a little. "So Chad's expensing fancy dinners and airfare to the same company that Conasauga is paying out the nose to. That's not a coincidence."

"No," Sam said. "So, what? Del can't send Lew after us, so he gets his lobbying firm to do it? Something about that feels off."

He tapped the link for the list of lobbyists and scrolled through the names: Adam Lugo, Nathalia Berger, Jameson Blair, Kenneth Nasta, Sarai Cline—

"Oh, hey—" Rufus paused midthought, glanced down, and crouched. He stood back up holding a gray tabby. Scratching under the bodega cat's chin, he continued, "Is that Nasta guy related to Jennifer Nasta? I keep getting her fucking reelection campaign texts, even when I report them as spam."

A new search showed that, yes, Kenneth Nasta was married to Jennifer Nasta—who happened to be a member of Congress, and who was currently serving on the House Defense Subcommittee.

"You have got to be fucking kidding me," Sam said.

Bodega Cat climbed up Rufus's chest and perched on his shoulder, tail wrapped around his neck.

"A Defense Subcommittee member who's doing business with her lobbyist husband," Rufus began, ticking the points off on his fingers. "Who, in turn, is doing business with Conasauga, who covered up a defense fiasco. Did I get that right?"

"This is a snake pit. And I bet if we start digging into Congresswoman Nasta, we'd find that Conasauga has contributed heavily to her election campaign, and that she, in turn, has been making sure Conasauga gets their share of the defense spending—contracts like Stonefish, for fuck's sake. So, Del and the colonel have a falling out. We're not sure why, but it seems like that woman, Evangeline, is involved somehow. Shareed too—she thought she could use Stonefish to squeeze some money out of them. No, hold on, let's do this in order."

"Starting with Stonefish," Rufus interjected.

Bodega Cat meowed loudly before jumping onto a nearby shelf of family-size chip bags, where it settled in for a late afternoon nap.

"Stonefish. It's a disaster. It's a disaster for Lew. It's a disaster for Colonel Bridges. And it's a disaster for Went. Went—" Sam wanted to say *dies*, but he forced himself to say, "—kills himself, and he gets blamed, and everyone moves on."

"Everyone moves on until Shareed," Rufus prompted next. "She's caught digging through old cases. She goes AWOL and calls you out of the blue. Why?"

"Because she's trying to get money. Out of me. Out of anybody. She needs it because she's already fucked herself over, and she's trying to score big before it all implodes. So, she calls me. She calls Evangeline. And it's no coincidence she drops Lew's name—I think she must have called him too, and that's how she got herself killed."

Rufus looked over his shoulder in the direction of the guy standing behind the counter, but he was absolutely transfixed by some video on his phone. Rufus said, "Shareed shows her hand to the wrong guy and it gets her killed. And now the convention is in full swing and out comes Del Jolly and Colonel Bridges."

"Right. And it's where everything gets messy. So, Del and the colonel disagree about something, and it sounds like Del is the one getting screwed—when we heard them at the bar, Del was desperate. And the colonel doesn't like that you and I are poking around; he sends Lew to get rid of us. Then Evangeline gets killed before we can get any straight answers out of her, and somebody kills the colonel. The next day, some assholes working for Civic Catalyst decide we need to go for a ride, and it turns out, they've got ties to a congresswoman whose husband has million-dollar ties to Conasauga. Which takes us back to my original question: what the fuck is going on?"

"The colonel's death is where everything goes topsy-turvy," Rufus said thoughtfully. He'd reached around Sam and quietly tugged free another snack bag of lime Takis from the shelf in front of them.

Sam didn't bother to point out that Rufus had been eating so many Takis lately that he was likely only a bag away from *becoming* one.

"There's an argument to be made," Rufus started, "that Del could want the colonel dead, but considering Del not only attended his panel at the Javits today, but was essentially tossed into the trunk of a car afterward by peoples unknown, I'm inclined to admit… he probably didn't pull the trigger." Rufus offered Sam the Takis a second time.

With a roll of his eyes, Sam took it. After a few crunches, he said, "So, some questions: who wanted Evangeline dead, and why? Who wanted the colonel dead, and why? And who wanted the whole Stonefish mess to come out, and why? I mean, it's been a long time. Why now?"

"I think another question we should consider is: who gave the go-ahead for Chad and Jarhead to come after us this morning?" Rufus asked. "Because I don't get the feeling they're associated with Del. Which means it was someone else. Should we be seriously looking at that connection Chad has with Civic Catalyst?"

"I think the fact that they're tied up with Conasauga means we have to seriously consider the possibility they have something at stake in this too, even if we don't know exactly what yet." Sam checked his phone again. "They've got a satellite office here. Big surprise, since Chad's a local. It's on—it looks like Pine and Water. Does that sound right?"

"A lobbyist company with a satellite office in the Financial District sounds very right," Rufus agreed. "Stereotypical, even." He flashed Sam a big grin. "Wanna go see if that's where Chad's been lying low all afternoon?"

CHAPTER
TWENTY-FOUR

Eight stops on the downtown A didn't sound like much, but in reality, it was still a thirty-five minute ride to get from Harlem to the water's edge of southern Manhattan. Thirty-five long minutes packed into a train like sardines in a tin can because it was the start of evening rush hour. They were shoulder-to-shoulder with way too many teenagers either performing showtime to an unenthusiastic audience or trying to upsell candy bars—the latter of which Rufus wondered might be a violation of some child labor law. And then there was that one dipshit at 59 Street-Columbus Circle who held the doors open for so long that the conductor shouted over the intercom: "I will get out of this fucking car and beat your ass if you don't let go of the goddamn doors!"

Business as usual in the New York City subway system.

Rufus had used the opportunity to catch a quick nap on Sam's shoulder. He'd drifted in that no man's land between sleep and awake, where rest could be obtained but he was still able to come around just as the train pulled into Fulton Street station. Leading the way up to street level, Rufus hunched his shoulders against the bitterly cold wind skimming off the water and roaring down the maze of tiny streets that defied the uptown grid system.

He moaned, "It's colder than a witch's tit down here." Rufus stuffed his hands into his jean jacket pockets, stamped his feet a few times, and turned around before inclining his head in one direction. "Pine Street is this way, I think."

Rufus and Sam wove around gaggles of men and women—probably senior finance staff leaving their high-paying Wall Street jobs for the day while interns and newly hired college graduates burned the midnight oil for peanuts. Turning off William and onto Pine—a one-way that felt more like an alleyway, what with the massive skyscrapers all but blotting out the sky—Rufus slowed as they came up on an imposing building of polished black stone and glass. To one side stood an open loading dock, a couple of guys bundled in enough Carhartt to be shooting an ad standing around on a smoke break.

Rufus asked with a curious inflection, "What's the floor number for the office—does their website say?"

Sam checked his phone. "Eighth floor."

"Follow me." Head down and hands still in his pockets, Rufus walked toward the loading dock with purpose, like he had somewhere to be, and just as two of the workers dropped their cigarette butts and started shoving each other—a bunch of hot air or an actual fight, Rufus couldn't yet determine—he slipped into the open doorway. He waited for Sam before heading deeper into the caverns of the building.

It smelled like cold cement and like exhaust and oil from nearby parked cars—most likely those of executives working in this high-rise office. The commercial overhead bulbs were bare and one flickered like a nervous tic.

Finding an elevator around one corner, Rufus jabbed the Up button and the doors immediately opened. They stepped inside, hit 8, and went up without any stops. A quiet ding welcomed them into a hallway of dark polished wood offset by light beige walls. A plaque on the opposite far wall specified Goodman, Goodman, and Goodman to the left, Civic Catalyst to the right.

"They should've called their company G3," Rufus commented, pausing to tap the plaque with his knuckle before walking toward the right.

"A real missed opportunity." Sam glanced left, then right. "It's a ghost town."

Rufus pointed to the bottom of the door, indicating a pale strip of light visible from inside. He whispered, "Someone's still working."

Outside the office of Civic Catalyst, Rufus took a deep breath, flexed his hand a few times to work the cold out of his joints, then pressed down on the door handle. Without a sound, it opened onto a small reception area with a desk, three chairs along the wall, an end table stacked with what Rufus assumed wealthy people read—*Wall Street Journal*, *The New Yorker*, *Martha Stewart Living*—and a fake potted plant with a wadded tissue stuck in it.

Down a hallway past the front desk were a number of internal rooms—private offices, most likely—their doors closed and no lights on. Rufus frowned at that, because he was certain he could hear a muffled conversation coming from nearby. He glanced sideways at Sam, and sure enough, the other man's gaze was locked on something in the distance, the concentration on his face suggesting they'd both heard the same thing.

Rufus pointed toward the right.

Sam shook his head and motioned left.

Rufus figured the guy who'd once been in active combat situations probably knew which direction a potential threat was coming from, so he obediently moved to the left. He pressed his back to the wall, stood on the balls of his feet, and slowly crept toward the farthest office.

This one didn't have its lights off.

Multiple voices—angry voices—filtered out from the partially open door. Rufus didn't wait to catch bits of the conversation, just grabbed Sam's arm and all but dragged him into a dark and unoccupied conference room.

"—talk to you for a moment?" The voice grew louder as the door swung open, and a wedge of light opened across the floor. Footsteps moved out into the hall—more than one man. The door shut again, and when the man began speaking again, his voice had shed its polite veneer. "What the fuck is wrong with you? I asked you to do one thing, and not only do you manage to fuck it up, but you fuck it up in broad fucking daylight. People were calling the police!"

"Mr. Nasta—" It took Rufus a moment before he thought, maybe, the voice belonged to Jarhead, the guy from the town car earlier that day.

At the same time, a stuffed-up voice said, "It's not our fault!"

Chad, Rufus guessed. With his broken nose.

"Shut up." Heavy breathing followed the words. "This is your mess; you're going to clean it up. And you're going to be goddamn grateful that I've got even bigger problems to deal with. Now get out of my sight."

Rufus looked at Sam and mouthed, "Chad."

Footsteps moved off down the hallway, but the man who'd been speaking remained where he was—taking those labored breaths only a few feet away. Then the sound came of the door opening again, and in a different voice, he said, "Sorry about that, Del, Jen. Are we all set? Del, why don't we get you out of here?"

"It's crucial that we all keep calm, keep quiet, until this storm passes," said the one woman—probably Jen. "Do you understand, Del?"

"I'm not an idiot." He emerged from the office, with a trim, dark-haired woman holding his arm. She was dressed in a blouse and navy slacks, her dark hair in a french braid. Her expression was unreadable. Rufus had seen a picture of her earlier on Sam's phone—she was Congresswoman Jennifer Nasta, and apparently she was tied up in this mess too. As they started down the hall, Del yanked his arm away. "And I do *not* appreciate how this was handled."

"I don't appreciate finding out you were in attendance at MoDe today for God and all the city to see. That's not how we stay quiet," Jen countered cooly, although her posture was indicative of a woman scorned. "And I told you to stay quiet, Del. Do I need to remind you *why* you're going to stay quiet?"

Del made a sputtering, wordless response.

"Do I need to remind you *why* you're going to do whatever I tell you to do?" Jen still hadn't raised her voice. "Speak up, Del."

It took several seconds before Del said, "No."

"Good. I'd hate to have to remind you."

Del shuffled along without responding, Jen at his side. The man who had been addressed as Mr. Nasta trailed after them without speaking.

Rufus was starting to sweat—central heat turned up too high, mixing with an adrenaline rush. His heart was pounding in his ears as he leaned close to Sam and whispered, "Let's follow."

The quiet voices of Del and Jen were farther down the hall now, on their way toward reception as Rufus and Sam slipped out of the conference room and moved cautiously in the same direction. Rufus confirmed the previously occupied office was indeed empty, then continued until they reached the long wall of previously closed doors.

One now stood ajar, the interior lights on.

Rufus took Sam's arm, moved to the same side of the hallway, and crept toward the door. The closer they got, the better Rufus could make out the nasally voice of Chad, probably talking to Jarhead. He stopped outside the room, crouched on one knee, and peered through the crack between door and frame.

"I'm good for it." That sounded like Jarhead. "You know I am. Come on, quit dicking me around."

"I can't eat on IOUs," Chad retorted.

Rufus rolled his eyes. *Amateur*.

"This is the last time, man. I'm sick of having to chase you down for payment." And Chad tossed a small, palm-sized baggy of what was so obviously coke across the desktop where he sat.

"Excuse me?"

Rufus startled so badly at the unexpected voice that he fell backward into Sam's legs before his ass hit the floor. He looked up to see Congresswoman Nasta, arms lightly crossed, painted fingernails tapping one bicep. Her presumed husband appeared beside her seconds later, looking far more irate than she did.

Ever the politician, she asked with polite severity, "Who're you?"

CHAPTER
TWENTY-FIVE

When Rufus hit Sam's legs, Sam was still in the process of turning toward the voice that had caught them by surprise. The result was that the impact, even though it was minor, put Sam off balance, and he stumbled.

At the same time, Kenneth Nasta shouted, "Security!"

Rufus scrambled clear of Sam's legs, and Sam caught himself on the wall.

That was when the door to Chad's office flew open. Jarhead moved faster than Sam expected—he already had a gun in his hand, and his quick glance seemed to take in the situation in a heartbeat. Then, while Sam was still steadying himself and Rufus was trying to get free, Jarhead bent, grabbed Rufus's coat, and hauled the redhead toward him.

Sam took a step, hand dropping toward his own gun.

Rufus squirmed.

Jarhead brought the muzzle of the gun to Rufus's temple.

Sam stopped.

Rufus stopped.

Chad appeared behind Jarhead a moment later. He looked like shit; even under the bandage, his broken nose looked so swollen that Sam doubted he could breathe through it, and he had two black eyes that were going to look twice as bad tomorrow. He had a gun in his hand too, but he looked like a kid brother, the way he peered over Jarhead's shoulder.

"Ok," Sam said. "Nobody needs to get hurt."

"What the fuck?" Jarhead said gleefully.

"Mr. Nasta," Chad said. "Mr. Nasta! We caught them!"

"You didn't catch them, you idiot," Mr. Nasta said. "We practically stepped on them. What the hell kind of security are you? Jesus, this is a cluster."

Jen Nasta hadn't said anything since her question, and she was still looking at them like she expected an answer.

"Tell him to point that gun somewhere else," Sam said. "We can sit down and talk about this."

"These are the ones?" Jen asked, but the question seemed to be for her husband.

He nodded.

"What in the hell are they doing here?"

Mr. Nasta shrugged. Sam didn't peg him for the brains of the operation.

"Tell him to—" Sam began again.

"I heard you," Jen said. "Who are you?"

"Sam Auden."

"Yes, and who *are* you, Mr. Auden?"

The question had the shape of a trap.

"Are you a journalist?" Jen asked.

"What?"

"Because let me tell you, you're finished. Your editor or your publisher or whoever I'm going to sue after this debacle, they're not going to be happy with you. This is private property. You're breaking and entering. Not to mention being very, very stupid."

Sam tried to come up with something, but nothing came. Adrenaline buzzed through him, making his hands tremble, and any kind of thought seemed a long way off.

"Who," Jen asked slowly, "are you?"

He said the first thing that came to mind: "We know about Stonefish."

Fear made her expression contract. Only for a moment. And only once. She was good, Sam thought, at putting it away. Good at hiding it. But it had been there. And he'd seen it.

"What does it matter?" her husband said. "Who cares who they are? You heard him—they know about Stonefish!"

This time, it wasn't fear. It was closer to rage. And this time, Jen Nasta didn't try to hide it. She turned on her husband, and when he saw her face, he shrank into his shitty little blazer so fast that the brass buttons quivered. She held him in her gaze for another heartbeat. And then she said to Chad, "Handle this."

Chad nodded.

As Jen Nasta and her husband moved off down the hallway, Sam tried to think of something to say.

"We have the emails," he called. "If anything happens to us, people are going to know."

The low light rendered her more as a shape than anything else, all the fine details eroded away, but she stopped and glanced back. And then she said, "Find out if that's true."

They turned a corner, and their footsteps died into silence.

"Here's what's going to happen," Chad said, still playing little brother behind Jarhead. "You're going to be real smart so nothing happens to your butt buddy here. Right?"

Sam nodded.

"Take a few steps back. Then I want you to turn around and put your hands behind your head."

Sam cut his eyes to Rufus.

Rufus's face was the color of dirty dishwater, his eyes wide with fear and wet with unshed tears, but he nodded at Sam.

Sam moved back, turned, and laced his fingers behind his head.

Shuffling sounds came, and then footsteps on carpet.

"Now this next part, don't get any ideas," Chad said. He was right behind Sam now. "I'm going to take this." Chad shoved Sam's coat out of the way and removed Sam's pistol from its holster. He beat a quick retreat, and from the office he'd just left came the sound of a desk drawer rattling open and then closed again. As Chad came back to the hallway, he said, "If you turn around, I'm going to shoot you. Then Shane's going to shoot the dyke."

"I'm not—" Rufus bit back any further offense.

"Clear?"

Sam nodded. Or he thought he did. His voice cracked when he made himself say, "Clear."

"Ok. Here we go. Straight out the door to the elevator."

Sam started toward the front of the office. He could hear Chad a few steps behind, and then the slightly uneven steps of Shane forcing Rufus along. As Sam walked, he looked for something, anything. But it was a hallway of closed doors, and there was nothing.

When they emerged into the small lobby at the front of the suite, the soft trickle of a desktop water feature sounded impossibly loud; Sam couldn't believe he hadn't heard it—hadn't paid attention to it—when they'd come this way before. He looked at the desk. There would be scissors, maybe even a letter opener. Hell, in a pinch, he could club this son of a bitch with a tape dispenser. But it was at least ten feet from the hallway to the desk, and before he had time to rummage through the drawers, Chad would shoot him in the back.

Then they were leaving the Civic Catalyst offices, moving into the corridor that led to the elevator. Nothing here except polished wood and the yellow film of fluorescent light—even less, if possible, than the last hallway. Not even a closed door. The buzz of the ballast probably wouldn't have bothered anyone else. Sam could feel it in his jaw.

In the polished metal of the elevator doors, his reflection was a greasy smear.

"Down," Chad said.

Sam pressed the button, and a moment later, the doors opened with a soft ding.

"This is where things get tricky," Chad said. "Nose in the corner. On your knees. Keep your hands where they are."

So, Sam knelt in the corner of the elevator. The metallic odor of the chrome rail and whatever polish they used made his eyes water. He was sweating more now, his shirt wet under his arms, his sides slick with it. He could smell that too. The car shifted slightly when Chad came aboard. And then again when Shane moved Rufus inside. Sam thought that, if he closed his eyes, he would recognize Rufus's breathing.

No one spoke, but the soft click of a button being depressed came through the silence. The car rocked slightly and then started down.

Think, Sam told himself.

They wouldn't stop at ground level; they had a guy on his knees, they had another guy with a gun to his head. They were going to the parking garage. And if it were Sam making the call, he'd shoot them there. In the garage. It would be empty. It would be dark. It would hold the sound of the shots. And when it was over, Chad and Shane would load them into a car and get rid of their bodies.

If they were going to do something, it had to be soon. In the elevator would be ideal. The tight space would actually make it easier, in some ways—easier to grapple, easier to control the field, easier to neutralize the advantage of the guns.

Except that as soon as Sam made a move, he and Rufus would get bullets in the head.

He wished he could see Rufus's face.

He wished he could say sorry. For getting him into this. For his—his mood, for lack of a better word, over the last few days. For all that shit about the city, for letting it fuck around inside the good thing they had. Sorry for answering Shareed's phone call, for getting fixated on Lew, for insisting they keep going even when bodies kept dropping—it wasn't rational. It was a memory, and his subconscious connecting dots.

"You're making a big mistake," Sam said.

Chad didn't say anything.

A flicker of doubt. Maybe this wasn't the cokehead amateur hour after all.

But Sam tried again anyway. "How much do you think she'd pay for those emails?"

Still nothing.

"You can have them if you let us go." His lips were so dry he thought they were cracking. "If you kill us, though, you get jack shit."

The elevator whined on its cable as it descended.

And then Sam heard it: the slight shift of weight. Eagerness and uncertainty and greed, all communicated through the tiniest movement of a body.

"She said to find out," Shane muttered, like Sam and Rufus might not hear him.

Chad's silence lasted longer.

But, it turned out, it *was* cokehead amateur hour.

"What emails?" he asked.

"Your boss rolled in the shit. And we've got the emails to prove it. We're the only ones who know where they are, aren't we, Rufus?"

"We—uh, yeah. We know where they are. Sucks for you guys, huh?" Rufus said, his voice mostly steady.

"Bullshit," Chad said.

"It's true," Sam said. He wanted to close his eyes now. Wanted to know, somehow, if Rufus knew. If what he'd heard in his voice, that catch, was confusion or understanding. "You heard her when we were up there."

"Dude," Shane said in that weirdly delusional whisper. "She told us to find out!"

"How 'bout a show of good faith?" Rufus interjected. "I got one of them on me. But only the one. I'll give it to you. It's in my pocket."

"Nice try—" Chad began. And then he barked, "No!"

The sound of movement. The crunch of bone hitting bone.

Sam launched himself to his feet. The only luck of the day was that Chad had turned to face Rufus and Shane. Shane had both hands pressed to his face. Blood bloomed between his fingers. Rufus staggered away from him. A mark on his forehead—red turning to white—suggested what had happened.

Then Chad started to bring his gun up.

Sam charged into him. He caught Chad's arm in one hand. With the other, he gripped the man's belt. Adrenaline made Sam's vision contract. He was only distantly aware of Chad's weight as he lifted the man off his feet, spun, and slammed him face first into the panel of the elevator car—he thought he heard Chad's already broken nose crumple again.

Chad's gun went off. The clap deafened Sam. Chad twisted, trying to get free. His head wobbled on his neck.

Sam slammed him against the panel again. Chad's struggles grew more disoriented. Shifting his focus, Sam hammered Chad's hand—the one holding the gun—against the chrome safety rail. On the third blow, he felt something break, and Chad's hand opened. The gun made a muffled thud when it hit the floor.

Sam dropped Chad and scooped up the gun. The elevator was tiny, but it felt like an eternity before he found Rufus. He was rubbing his forehead, a gun in his hand, scowling down. Shane lay on the floor, one hand over his broken nose, the other cupping his 'nads, moaning.

The elevator slowed. Stopped. Settled.

The doors opened with a ding. On the other side, bare concrete met them, and the smell of oil, and lights spaced far apart. A long way off, Sam thought he could hear traffic.

He grabbed Rufus, and they ran.

CHAPTER
TWENTY-SIX

Hotel 10 was actually located on East Eleventh Street, not Tenth, but it was several neighborhoods north of the Financial District—which was, in Rufus's opinion, the fact to focus on. Tourists would probably refer to Hotel 10 as a "classy hostel," but it was more like an upscale YMCA. The two-star joint had existed for as long as Rufus could remember. He'd always assumed it had once been a rich family's home during the nineteenth century, surviving the test of time only because it'd been successfully chopped up into two dozen rentable rooms. Such extreme changes to its interior had left the public hallways of each floor almost maze-like in their appearances, with some so crooked and narrow that a grown man's shoulders would rub either wall as he made for his room. And the low wattage bulbs—which made it easier to hide torn wallpaper and hundred-year-old scuffed floors—cast such an ethereal glow Rufus felt almost certain he'd turn a corner and see Alice chasing after a white rabbit, and it'd turn out that he was in Wonderland this whole time.

But no. This wasn't Wonderland.

This was New York.

And Hotel 10 might have been trippy, but it was also cheap, short-staffed, with no questions asked.

Opening the door to room 7 on the fourth floor, Rufus made a sound in the back of his throat. The flowery green wallpaper across the six-sided room, the threadbare, pink paisley bedspread, and the maroon shade on the lone window was really an assault on the senses. A cheap shelving unit had been installed on the wall opposite the foot of the bed, allowing for barely enough space to squeeze between the two. It was loaded with a small television, microwave, and desktop telephone. Sitting atop the microwave was a pile of folded towels and two tiny complimentary bars of soap. Beside the furniture was a sink. The actual bathroom was back the way they'd come and shared with the rest of the fourth-floor guests.

Rufus pulled his beanie off and turned around as Sam closed the door behind them. "I like it," he started, trying his hardest for a smile. "It's… very colorful."

"It's definitely that."

Rufus caught his reflection in the small mirror above the sink. He leaned down for a better look, then straightened and asked, "Does my forehead have a bruise, or is that just the lighting in here?"

Sam reached up. His thumb traced a line of sensitive skin, and then he bent and kissed Rufus's forehead. "It's a bruise, baby. You knocked his block off."

"I don't think I did it right."

"You did it right. It hurts like a bitch any way you do it."

Rufus stared up at his boyfriend's deep brown eyes. So hard, so soft, so critical, so beautiful. "They were gonna kill us, Sam."

Sam let out a shaky breath and nodded.

Rufus shrugged out of his jacket and sweatshirt before dropping onto the foot of the bed. Tiredly, he gave the mattress a light inviting pat.

Sam turned himself out of his coat more slowly. When he sat, the bed sank under his weight, and Rufus rocked into him. He ran a hand over Rufus's head, brushing his fingers through Rufus's hair.

"I'm not naïve," Rufus said as he put his head on Sam's shoulder. "I know most politicians don't give a damn about the people they represent. But until now, the closest I've gotten to actual 'government conspiracy' was a few dirty cops."

After a moment, Sam laughed softly. "That is not where I thought this was going." He was quiet then. The rise and fall of his body with each breath was pleasantly rhythmic. "I don't know if it's a government conspiracy so much as a conspiracy involving a lot of government types." Another pause came, more considering. "She freaked out about Stonefish."

"Because the whole thing was a cover-up," Rufus answered. He slumped a bit lower so he could wrap his arms around Sam in a sideways embrace. "A cover-up means you're conspiring to conceal the truth. Ergo, government conspiracy."

"So, what do we know? She's on the Defense Subcommittee. Her husband's a lobbyist with ties to Conasauga. They picked Del up off the street like he was a sack of potatoes, and even if he didn't like it, he didn't tell them to fuck off. I mean, it's not hard to follow the thread—Conasauga pays her husband, she makes sure

Conasauga gets contracts, and Stonefish threatens to send everything to fuck, but they manage to cover it up. Why pick up Del like that, though?"

"They kept telling Del to stay calm," Rufus added. "Do they think he's a loose cannon? Or loose-lipped?"

"Del definitely lost his cool with the colonel when we saw them in the hotel. He seemed desperate, and desperate people do stupid things." Sam grimaced. "We're missing a piece of the puzzle."

Rufus picked a bit of lint from Sam's shirt. "I hate that we didn't have a chance to speak with Evangeline. It's like an itch on my brain, you know? There's a reason she's dead and Del's not."

"And I don't think her friends at Conasauga are going to want to help us."

"You mean, if she *had* any friends besides My-Eyes-Are-Up-Here Anson. She didn't come off as the most likable—"

"That guy." And then Sam said, "Holy shit. That guy. He was all up in her business, right? And he wanted to talk to us at the conference center? Wouldn't get out of the fucking way when we were trying to catch Del."

Rufus's light-colored brows crept up to his hairline. "You think he knows—what? About her death? About Del, maybe? Or about Evangeline's work relationship with Del?"

"I don't know. But if he's got something to say, maybe we should hear it."

"I don't have his phone number," Rufus replied. "Do you?"

"No."

Rufus stood up. He tried to pace, but having to step over Sam's legs just to get between the bed and the entertainment stand brought that to an end pretty quickly.

"We could call the general number of Conasauga or—*oh*! Hey! You know LinkedIn, right? It's like Facebook but for finance bros?"

"I don't think they bill themselves as Facebook for finance bros."

"What I mean is, the kind of people who were at the Javits are the same people who'd have LinkedIn profiles. I'm pretty sure you get instant messages on that platform."

"That's actually a good idea." He frowned. "I don't have an account, though. Do you?"

Rufus shrugged. "I can make one."

A smile crooked across Sam's face. "Now *that* I'd like to see."

"What's that supposed to mean?" Rufus yanked his burner from his pocket. "I'm going to make Rufus—no—*Devon*. Devon MacDougal. He's an up-and-coming young exec thirsty for fresh opportunities and new professional contacts." Rufus navigated LinkedIn's web page and started creating a new account. "Most recent job title... hmm.... External Vice President of Communications. That sounds good. Hey, do you think Devon would have been in a fraternity?"

"Obviously he would have been in a fraternity. Alpha Tau Asshole, I think."

"Anson isn't going to answer messages from a brother of the Alpha Tau Asshole Chapter." Rufus took several more minutes to finish bullshitting his way through some recent job placements and academic achievements and was pretty impressed with his ability to use a lot of action verbs that really said a whole heap of nothing, once you deconstructed Devon's profile. He briefly considered whether this newly-found skill was something he could monetize, then Rufus offered Sam the phone.

"What does 'Innovated customer-oriented experience' mean?"

"Sounds sexy, doesn't it?"

Sam tossed him the phone. "You need a picture."

Rufus raised the cell and quickly snapped a photo of Sam. "Gosh, what a scowl," he murmured. He cropped the picture before uploading it. It took less than a minute before he found Anson's profile. "Found him! Devon's gonna invite him out for a beer, ok?"

Eyebrows raised, Sam said, "What's Devon's endgame here?"

"To get some nookie."

Sam did not look amused.

"I'm kidding. Geez. I'm gonna say there's a great networking opportunity—a popup event, I think they're called." Rufus turned, drew aside the shade on the window to take a look outside, then said, "It's happening conveniently across the street from us at the Public House. Once he's there, we can try to pull some intel about Evangeline outta him. Boom. Message sent. Let's see if Anson lives on his phone like the hungry little Regional Director of Business Development that he is."

"Perfect," Sam said. "We can eat while we wait."

"Wanna treat Devon to something nice?"

CHAPTER
TWENTY-SEVEN

The Public House must have been moderately new. It was reasonably clean, without the patina of grime that a real dive had. No split upholstery or wobbly tables. The theme, apparently, was light bulbs. It seemed like every fucking inch of space was studded with light bulbs. Even the risers on the stairs to the mezzanine had light bulbs. Dim, sure. Nothing bright enough to break the ambience. But it looked like Thomas Edison's wet dream, and it was loud—loud with voices, loud with glass and flatware, loud with music. When the beat dropped on the house track, Sam could feel it in his teeth.

A lot of Sam's ill will went away, though, when he smelled beer and cheeseburgers.

They lucked into one of the tables on the mezzanine,

right against the railing, which gave them an eagle-eye view of the pub's entrance. No sign of Anson, but then, it might take him a while. Or he might change his mind. Might not come at all.

Their waiter was young, blond, and so thin that when he stretched to set a coaster in front of Sam and his shirt rode up, Sam could see his ribs. He'd wanted Sam to see, Sam figured. He had little silver hoops all the way up his right ear, and he looked at Rufus like he was wondering whether he could push him off the mezzanine and get away with it.

Sam ordered a cheeseburger. Well, a double. With fries. They had Stella on tap, so he ordered that.

"I'll have the same—oh, a Stella? Stella's fine. I'll get everything he ordered," Rufus told the waiter while motioning to Sam.

With a little wiggle of his behind, the waiter left.

"When he comes back," Rufus started, leaning to one side and watching the waiter go. "Switch glasses with me."

"I think he bared his teeth before he left."

"Yeah, I'm pretty sure he's gonna spit in my beer."

"The joys of civilization."

When his phone buzzed, Rufus fished his cell free from his pocket. He glanced at the screen before rolling his eyes. "Another Jen Nasta, Original American Patriot, text. I can confidently say she won't be getting my vote next year." Rufus set his phone to one side. He didn't say anything else as they sat and waited. Eventually, he yanked off his beanie and his shock of red hair was a little staticky. Rufus pushed aside utensils rolled up in a paper napkin, fiddled with his coaster, then suddenly blurted out, "I know you said we'd figure it out, and I know we will, because you don't lie to me about that kind of stuff, but I can't stop thinking about how much you don't like it here."

Downstairs, a glass broke, and screams—startled, excited, full of drunken hilarity—rang out. A few people looked up; not everyone. At the table next to Sam and Rufus, a man was glued to his phone. His wife was trying to kill a bottle of wine all by herself.

"I was thinking about that," Sam said. "Not thinking, I guess. I mean—" He flattened his hands on his thighs. He focused on the feeling of gravity. The way his body felt solid, anchored, real. "In the elevator, with those guys—" When he tried again, he had to screw his voice down against the rush of emotion. "If that had been it—" He chafed his hands against his jeans. "You matter. The rest of it—I don't know why I've been such an asshole. I'm sorry. I'm sorry for a lot of things."

"You were in the hospital," Rufus said with a shrug. "And you've had unresolved acute trauma. Dr. Donna says that's when it's from a single specific incident that gets thrown in your face. You've had valid reasons to be moody."

"Moody." Their waiter brought their beers. When Sam ignored what was probably meant to be an irresistible smile, the blond boy scowled and flounced away. "That's part of it, sure. And I know I've been—adjusting, I guess. But the medication is helping." It was like trying to find his way through the dark, he thought. Even with all those fucking light bulbs. "I don't know what I'm saying. I guess I'm saying, again, I'm sorry. For getting you into this. For—" He couldn't help a wry smile. "—my unresolved acute trauma. I want to do better. I want to find a way to make this work. I love you." And then, because it popped into his head. "Maybe I should get a job."

Rufus pursed his lips a little, like he'd just taken a bite of something sour. But thoughtfully, he said, "I can make you a very impressive LinkedIn profile for your résumé."

"Maybe not *that* kind of job," Sam said with a laugh.

"But I don't know. I feel like I do better—like *we* do better—when we're doing something. It's been a long time since I've had some structure to my life. After the Army, I was sick of structure, and then, when I wasn't so angry, there wasn't any reason for it. But now there's you. Maybe I'd feel a little more settled here if I—" He felt like he was at the end of his words, so he gave another of those crooked smiles and said, "If I wasn't sitting in the apartment all day."

Rufus reached under the table and gave Sam's thigh a squeeze. "If I'm not allowed to rot in bed all day, neither are you. I think you're probably onto something about structure."

Before Sam could reply, movement at the door caught his eye. Anson stood there in his yuppie uniform: button-up, trousers, polished oxfords. He'd added a wool overcoat that, Sam was willing to bet, had cost somewhere in the four figures. It was kind of reassuring to know that, even when the rest of the world got fucked, Anson was always going to be a tool.

"God, look at him," Sam said. "He's trying to figure out which group is the pop-up whatever the fuck you told him about."

"It's a networking event for sales executives," Rufus said heavy-handedly, but from the corner of his eye, Sam saw Rufus quickly wiping his face with the back of his hand. "Give your pal a wave. It's your face on Devon's profile, after all."

When Anson scanned the crowd again, Sam held up a hand. Anson must have spotted the gesture because he glanced up. Then he stared up at them. He gave another look around, clearly starting to tumble to what was going on as he shrank down inside his coat. Then, shooting furtive glances in every direction, he started toward the stairs.

At their table, he did a final, disappointed check—as though a group of white, bro-y guys might jump out and surprise him—and then said, "There isn't any pop-up networking event, is there?"

"Sorry," Sam said. "Grab a seat."

Anson pulled a free chair over and dropped into it. "What the hell was that earlier? I was trying to talk to you, and you threw my phone!"

"Did I?" Rufus asked, hand to his chest in mock-confusion. "You must have me confused with another redheaded punk with no ass."

Anson gave him a dirty look and turned to Sam. "What the fuck is going on, man? First, you're asking about Evangeline, and then she—" His voice dropped into a stage whisper. "—dies." Then, back at full volume. "And then the next day, everyone's talking about how Colonel Bridges—" His voice dropped again. "—died."

"You don't have to whisper," Sam said. "They know they're dead. Well, assuming they know anything."

Anson stared at him, apparently incapable of processing that.

Rufus leaned across the table, snapped his fingers in front of Anson's face, and asked, "So what kinda work did Evangeline have you doing?" Seemingly trying to loosen Anson up, Rufus asked next, "Were you a personal assistant or something?"

"What? Dude." Outrage left him flatfooted for a moment. "I'm, like, the Regional Director of Business Development."

"*Oh*." More feigned surprise on Rufus's part. "Not a Regional Director of Titties?"

Anson paled. His lips parted, but he didn't say anything.

"Holy shit," Sam said. "You were boinking?"

"No, we—" But if anything, his eyes got wider. "I—"

"Hey, hey, I get it," Rufus interjected. "I mean… not personally, do I get it, but they *looked* big and pillowy. So what was your end game? Tap the boss and get promoted to Director of Regional Directors?" Rufus slumped forward, elbows resting on the tabletop as he stared at Anson expectantly.

"Big and pillowy," Sam said under his breath.

"Hey, man, not cool!" Although, to be fair to Rufus, Anson did sit up a little straighter. "Evangeline was smart. She was super good at what she did. And we, like, respected each other." If he was still worried about being seen with them, he must have forgotten, because he puffed up inside his coat as he said, "She even asked me my opinions and stuff."

"That's what we wanted to talk to you about," Sam said. "You know what happened to Evangeline, that wasn't an accident, right?"

Anson squirmed in his seat. "No, people are saying—"

"Just like what happened to Colonel Bridges wasn't an accident. You don't accidentally fall off a balcony inside a crowded convention center, Anson. And you don't accidentally get shot in your own hotel room. Someone killed them. I think you might know who."

"What—why—no!" But the little sales bro was so white he looked like he might pass out.

Rufus straightened. "Don't make me walk you through deep breathing exercises, Anson. Why don't you tell us what you know? Even if it's nothing big. It won't go beyond this table."

"But I don't know anything! Oh God. Did somebody say I did? I don't! I'm, like, innocent!"

"Innocent of what?" Sam asked.

It was practically a wail: "Everything!"

Rufus held up both hands in defense. "Hey, it's cool. I'm innocent of everything too. Never lied, cheated, or stole in my entire life. You can ask my mother."

It was a good thing, Sam thought, he hadn't been taking a drink.

"You wanted to talk to us earlier today," Sam said. "Why?"

More squirming. More shifting. He even glanced around again, and Sam realized, with something like wonder, that Anson actually believed someone had followed him.

"Well, I was thinking, you know, just, um, a possibility, but what if it *wasn't* an accident? Evangeline, I mean." And then, voice even lower: "What if someone did it on purpose? And you were asking about Evangeline, and I thought maybe you knew."

Sam wasn't sure what other option there was, but now didn't seem like the right moment to derail Anson. He nodded and said, "Why would someone have wanted to hurt Evangeline?"

Anson frowned as though he didn't understand why they didn't understand. "Because she was leaving."

"Leaving the company?" Rufus asked hesitantly.

Nodding, Anson said, "Oh yeah. She hadn't said anything yet—I mean, only to me, because, you know, we respected each other—"

"Totally," Rufus agreed, somehow keeping a straight face.

"—but New Haven wanted her bad. They poached her, and she was waiting for the right time to tell everyone." He thought about it and added, "Probably because they were going to be so pissed that she was taking Colonel Bridges with her—"

"*Bro*," Rufus said, long and low. "Did Evangeline tell

you that? Specifically?"

"Tell me what?"

It looked to Sam that Rufus's façade nearly fell, but he managed to clarify, without a hint of irritation, "Did Evangeline tell you that the colonel was following her to this new job?"

"Oh. Yeah, I mean, she was kind of pissed about it because the guys at New Haven made the offer contingent on that, and she was like, I'm valuable because of who I am, not because of my client list, and I was like, maybe you aren't, but I mean, I didn't say it out loud."

Jesus Christ, Sam thought. And then he asked, "New Haven? Like, Yale?"

"Huh?"

"Who's New Haven?"

"Oh. New Haven Security. Why'd you think it was Yale?"

"Don't mind him, he's been salty ever since Yale rejected his college application," Rufus explained as he put a hand on Sam's shoulder. "Those SAT scores are a real bitch. So. Do you think some douche at Conasauga found out?"

Anson licked his lips. "They wouldn't *kill* her."

He didn't say it, but behind the words, Sam heard the question: *would they?*

"Would it be a big deal if Colonel Bridges had gone with Evangeline? Was he in charge of major purchases, that kind of thing?"

"Oh, yeah, definitely. That it would be a big deal. It's kind of complicated. It's not like he could authorize huge purchases on his own, but in this business, it's all about connections."

"And the colonel was a good guy to know?"

Anson nodded.

Rufus interrupted, "Uncle Sam's all about antitrust laws…. But I bet Conasauga could handle some healthy competition, right? Mr. Regional Director of Business Development?"

"Um, maybe?"

"That's not exactly inspiring," Sam said.

"I mean, it's not like there are a lot of people buying their own personal tactical vehicles. You've got to get those government contracts."

"What are we talking here? If Evangeline and the colonel hadn't died?"

Anson shrugged. "Probably the same thing that's going to happen now. Mr. Jolly, he's the president, he knows some people. But it's going to be a lot harder." He sat back, mouth turned down. "That's why it was such a bummer this wasn't a real networking event."

Sam frowned. "You think Conasauga is going to go under?"

"I think I don't want to stick around to find out. Look, man, I told you what I know. So, like—what do I do? Should I go to the police?" He looked ready to cry. "Is this, like, witness protection stuff?"

"Uh." Sam couldn't help it. "That's probably a better question for the police."

"I wouldn't know anything about the police or law, because I'm just an innocent civilian," Rufus began, "but between us… *bro*… get out of New York. Consider selling something less dangerous. Like used cars or lollipops. Ok?"

"Right," Anson breathed. "Right. Get out of New York. Right."

"Phone number," Sam said, "in case we have more questions. And if you think of anything else, let us know.

On LinkedIn."

Anson tossed a business card onto the table and scuttled out of the pub.

"Jesus," Sam said. "I'm surprised his underwear didn't fly off."

Rufus let out a long groan, slumping back in his chair. "It's hard to play good cop when the target is so dumb."

"It's hard to do anything when they're that dumb. What happened to our food?"

That was when the waiter brought it; it happened like that sometimes. Sam asked for another Stella, and this time, he didn't get a smile. But the burger was hot, and the fries were crispy, and that was better than a smile.

Rufus had eaten half of his burger in about two, maybe two and a half bites, before he asked around a mouthful of food, "Del's in hot water financially if the colonel leaves, right?"

"Yeah. And the colonel *has* left. Permanently. So, Conasauga is in trouble. Which raises the question: if the colonel leaving was such a problem, why would Del kill him? I mean, it doesn't solve the problem. If anything, it guarantees he's going to have a problem."

Rufus was in the midst of sneaking several fries off Sam's plate and onto his own when Sam concluded his train of thought. Rufus jerked his hand back, wiped his fingers on his napkin, and said, "I'm willing to admit that it's now tough to swallow my killing-in-the-heat-of-the-moment pill when I know that New Haven was doing a little headhunting."

"The timing," Sam said and stopped for another fry. "That bothers me too. I mean, if you're going to kill her for high treason, or whatever the corporate speak is for stealing the golden goose, why do it in a convention center? And why this weekend? I know I'm hammering on Stonefish, but think about it: we know Shareed contacted her. We know she and the colonel were done with Conasauga. Del was panicking. Doesn't it make sense that it's all tied together somehow?"

Rufus finished his cheeseburger in two more bites. He downed what was left of his beer before giving Sam a look that suggested he might have had an upset stomach, which didn't make sense, considering Rufus ate like he was a trash compactor. "I don't want you to puff your chest out or give me any 'I told you sos' or anything like that. But I'm now wondering, where's Lew been all day?"

"God, do we want to know? I'm surprised he didn't have his nose up Jen Nasta's skirt."

"That's what I mean, though. When we first saw him, he was talking with Colonel Bridges at the Conasauga panel. Just two guys who knew about Stonefish. But since then, there's been three murders, an abduction—" Rufus leaned in and lowered his voice to whisper, "—a fucking Congresswoman is involved, and Lew's known to orbit around these people. What if his orbit crosses over, you know? Like Pluto invading Neptune's space. I'm not saying he's suddenly offed three people, but that… maybe I owe you an apology for writing him off as innocent so quickly."

"No, you were right. I was so fixated on Lew, I missed a lot of stuff." Sam drew a deep breath and poked at his half-eaten burger. "But I think, now, we need to figure out where Lew fits in all this."

"I think we need to do more than that," Rufus answered. "I think we should try talking to him again."

CHAPTER
TWENTY-EIGHT

Rufus unlocked room 7. The ominous red light of the digital alarm clock boldly declared the time to only be 8:29 p.m. When he switched the overhead on, the hellish glow slinked away like a thoroughly chastised dog. The whole day—the fight on the street, the chase for Del, the sleuthing around Harlem, and nearly getting his head blown off—it'd all finally caught up with Rufus on their short walk from the Public House back to Hotel 10. He was mildly horrified by the notion that he seemingly couldn't keep up with death and danger like he once had, but when Rufus considered the second beer, side order of onion rings, as well as the fries he'd been steadily pilfering from Sam during dinner, it kind of made sense why he was ready to turn in the same time as nerds with a day job.

Maybe he was finally too old to mix fried food with murder.

Flopping onto the bed, Rufus said as Sam closed the door, "I think I have indigestion."

"Maybe it was those bonus fries you stole."

Rufus sat up on his elbows. "You saw that?"

Sam flashed a smile as he shrugged out of his coat.

"Why didn't you say something? Like, Rufus, stop eating my fries."

"Because you're cute when you think you're getting away with something."

"I get away with a lot." Rufus sat up the rest of the way in order to pull his jacket and sweatshirt off. He added, for clarification purposes, "And I'm *always* cute, Mr. Auden."

"Always, huh?"

Rufus tossed his beanie at Sam. "Do you think otherwise?"

"Nope." He smoothed a hand over Rufus's staticky hair. "I particularly like this look."

"What look?"

"This one," Sam said and kissed him.

Rufus grabbed Sam's t-shirt in both hands and pulled him down on top. He wrapped his legs around Sam's hips, keeping his boyfriend—and God did *boyfriend* feel like champagne bubbling in his gut—pinned to his own body. Sam pressed kisses along his jaw. One arm wrapped around Rufus, pulling him closer, while the other worked its way under Rufus's shirt.

"I don't have any lube," Rufus said between kisses. "But we—we can still do something, right?"

Sam's answer was a deep rumble as he scraped his stubble along Rufus's neck. He lowered Rufus to the bed, freed his arm, and then set to work turning Rufus out of his shirt. His own shirt was next: hands crossing to grab it at the hem, then yanking it off in a quick, economical movement. He bent over Rufus again, one hand palming Rufus's belly, then riding up his chest as Sam bent to kiss him again.

"Fuck, you're so hot." Rufus gave the button of his jeans a rough tug. "Take these off."

With a mock grimace, Sam leaned back. He undid the button on Rufus's jeans. The fly was next. Then he grabbed the jeans and pulled them off, exposing gray briefs. Rufus's dick pressed against the cotton, and the cold air made his skin pebble. He shivered as Sam dragged the briefs down, making Rufus's dick bob. Then Sam scooted back and rolled onto his back long enough to kick his jeans free. He'd gone commando, like usual, and his dick was hard, jutting out and up, bouncing slightly as Sam straddled Rufus again and bent to take one nipple in his mouth.

Rufus yelped unexpectedly before smacking a hand over his mouth. He snort-laughed. "S-sorry." He put one arm around Sam's neck and the other across his muscular back, pressing Sam down so that not even a single atom could exist between their bodies. He whispered Sam's name, kissed his mouth, urged him closer still, found their rhythm, and it was good.

So good.

Rufus wasn't even self-conscious anymore about his tendency to finish in record time. He just allowed himself to exist in the moment, to soak up the touch and sweat and affection and burn, and thank himself for hanging on another day when that sometimes felt impossible to do.

Because Sam was always worth one more day.

CHAPTER
TWENTY-NINE

By late afternoon the next day, the crowd at the Javits was even smaller. Smartly dressed men and women still filled the convention center, but it was—according to the program—the last day of the conference, and in every face, Sam could see the fatigue of days spent moving from booth to booth, panel to panel, social hour to networking event to keynote speaker, only to have their nights filled up with mandatory dinners and drinks. Not that he'd ever had to do any of it himself, but it didn't take much of an imagination.

A quick glance at the map led them to the concierge desk on the ground floor. The woman at the desk was probably in her twenties: a blue dress, dark hair in a bob, a name tag that said ANTARA. She smiled as they approached. It was such a good smile, she didn't even really need to ask, "Welcome to the Javits Center. How can I help you?"

"We need to page someone at the conference. Uh, one of the conferences. The MoDe US Expo."

She nodded along as he spoke and then said, "I'm so sorry, sir, but we can't page individual guests."

"You can't or you won't?" Sam asked.

"I'm very sorry. We can provide a visual page on the directories. And you can ask the expo organizers if they have an online guide or similar platform where they might be able to message the attendee."

"Just to be clear," Sam said, "you can't, or you won't?"

"All right, killer, stand down," Rufus warned, patting Sam's chest before giving his arm a tug. "She won't do it because she can't."

Sam let Rufus lead him away. He eyed the woman at the desk, who was—politely—pretending to ignore him. "Who the fuck doesn't do complimentary guest pages?"

"This is New York, babe. Nothing's complimentary."

"What are the chances Lew's going to see a visual page, whatever the fuck that is? Or that we can get somebody at the expo to try to contact him?"

"Probably not great," Rufus agreed. He was still holding on to Sam's arm. "But I do have friends in high-up places."

"Oh yeah?"

"I can give Erik a call and let him know about Chad dealing coke from inside the offices of Civic Catalyst. I think that might be worth a little favor in return."

"About time Erik made himself useful."

It didn't take long. Rufus got Erik on the phone— Sam refused to think of him as his *cop-daddy*, no matter how many times Rufus used the phrase—and after some haggling, he disconnected with a smile. About two minutes later, a page for Lew Frazer blared over the convention center's speakers. Behind her desk, Antara leveled a death look at Sam. He didn't *think* she knew he'd been behind the page, but then again, it sure looked like she did.

"Let's find somewhere we can wait," Sam said.

The open floor plan of the convention center didn't offer a lot of places for concealment, so Sam and Rufus ended up near the doors, where people seemed to cluster. Some of them chatted in loose knots, while others were on their phones, waiting for a friend or an Uber or something. Their voices bounced back from the glass, echoing, and the heat of the bodies, the smell of slush melting into high-traffic mats, it all pressed in on Sam. He took slow, deep breaths through his mouth, phone out in front of him like he was reading something, and scanned the crowd.

After a surprisingly short time, Lew emerged from the crowd. He looked like shit—his face was puffy, his crew cut was in disarray, even though it seemed impossible with hair that short, and his color was bad. He was dressed in rumpled civvies, and he moved, to put it bluntly, with his head on a fucking swivel.

Sam nudged Rufus and started across the lobby. He made for a point on the far side, so that his trajectory wouldn't put him on a direct course with Lew. People noticed things like that. The animal part of the brain noticed things like that. Sam kept his eyes on his phone, with Lew in his peripheral vision. Lew stood at the desk, arguing with Antara about something in a way that looked like it was going to send the young woman into not-very-concierge-like behavior. Another fifteen feet. All Sam had to do was get close enough to grab Lew before he could run. Then he'd march him—

As Sam glanced up, looking for a convenient place to

talk to Lew, movement directly ahead of him caught his eye.

It was hard to tell who looked worse—Chad or Shane. Chad's arm hung in a sling, and a cast wrapped from his hand to his elbow. He also wore one of those cervical collars, and it made it look like he was stretching his neck out too far; there was no way it was comfortable. Shane's nose was taped and splinted, and he had the holy mother of a black eye. Well, two black eyes. To judge from how he was squinting and not too steady, he also had a concussion—another point for Rufus. Like Chad, his gaze was fixed on Lew.

What the fuck, Sam thought, were they doing here?

Disbelief made him falter. It was only for a moment, and then his body recovered, and his pace smoothed out again. But it happened at exactly the wrong time, as Lew was turning away from the concierge desk, disgust scribbled across his features. He locked eyes on Sam. The color washed out of his face, and he turned and ran.

Sam sprinted after him.

At the same time, so did Chad and Shane.

"Rufus!" Sam shouted, and all he could do was hope Rufus understood what he was asking.

Ahead of him, Lew slid through the crowd near the doors. He didn't shout or shove. He didn't make any noise, although maybe that was because of the blood rushing in Sam's ears. Lew moved like a snake, and he was getting away.

Sam *did* shout. "Move! Move! Get out of the fucking way!"

Men and women squawked and shuffled and looked around. They reminded him of a flock of birds too dumb to care as a hunter started picking them off. Pheasants, Sam wanted to say.

He clipped one lady with his shoulder, and she screamed. A wide-eyed man in a fedora half-fell out of Sam's way. Then he reached the doors. Checking the crash bar with his hip, he spared a glance back for Rufus.

The redhead had body-slammed Chad to the ground, who was howling in pain as he was pinned, bad arm against the linoleum floor. Rufus scrambled over Chad's prone body, holding his neck brace with one hand while grabbing at Shane with his other. He caught the back of Shane's jacket and yanked, but the other man remained on his feet, kept moving, actually pulled Rufus along for a foot or two, before he tore free and broke into a run after Sam—after Lew.

Then Sam was plunging into the cold, weak daylight. He spun, trying to catch sight of Lew, and—

Hands caught him by the coat and spun him. Sam caught a glimpse of Lew's face as he bum-rushed Sam toward the street. It wouldn't have worked if he hadn't been off balance from turning around. It still might not have worked if the sidewalk hadn't been icy. But Sam's feet went out from under him, and all he could do was Scooby Doo the soles of his shoes against the frozen concrete, trying to get purchase, as Lew hurled him into traffic.

Sam stumbled, caught his balance, and was hit by a car.

It was a tap, really. Barely enough to jar him. Sam steadied himself with one hand on the hood. A wide-eyed kid who looked barely sixteen stared back at him from behind the wheel of the Audi. Horns blatted as traffic began to back up.

Sam gave the kid a wave. The kid waved back, eyes growing wider.

By the time Sam got to the sidewalk, Lew was halfway down the block. Shane wasn't far behind him. They moved down the crowded sidewalk like an arrow, parting the crowd behind them, leaving furious, shouting people in their wake. Sam started after them, trying to ignore the throbbing heat in his hip and hamstring, but he could already tell it was a lost cause. Sam had the advantage of an already cleared path, but Lew was faster, and he had too much of a lead. Unless he slipped and fell, which didn't seem likely, he'd lose Sam sooner or later.

Shane seemed to reach the same conclusion because he stopped running. Then he pushed back his coat, grabbed a gun from his waistband, and started firing at Lew.

One. Sam counted the shots as he broke into a run again. Two, three—

Lew slewed sideways. His feet went out from under him, and he rolled across the sidewalk.

—four—

The fuckhead was still shooting. The angry pedestrians had dissolved into a screaming, fleeing mob.

—five—

"Stop!" Sam shouted. And then, because it came to him: "Police!"

It was hard to believe Shane heard him over the chaos, but his head whipped around, and he took off at a run.

Distantly, Sam registered a minor miracle—none of the bystanders seemed to have been hit. Maybe because of the slanting light of sunset and the deep shadows. Maybe just luck. But that thought was peripheral; Sam's focus was on Lew, and he sprinted toward him. He lay on the sidewalk, and for a moment, he was so still that Sam thought he'd stopped breathing. Blood darkened his jeans, seeping outward from where the bullet had sliced open the side of his thigh. Not life threatening, although it probably hurt like a motherfucker. Scrapes and cuts on Lew's face and head suggested the fall had been even nastier than it looked; if he was in danger, it was from that more than the gunshot wound. Even as Sam performed the field triage, Lew raised his head and moaned.

"Fucking shit" seemed to be the extent of what he had to say.

"*Sam!*" Rufus was shouting, practically screaming, from farther down the sidewalk. He came running toward the two so fast he nearly plowed into them. "Oh my God, are you ok?" He raised his phone, hand shaking. "Do I call Erik again?"

Sam shook his head as he caught Lew's arm and dragged him upright. Lew let out a sharp cry; with the foot traffic still fleeing from the shooting, the sound echoed up and down the empty block. As soon as Sam had him upright, Lew started to fold, but Sam shook him and said, "Stay on your fucking feet." Then, to Rufus, he said, "No." Sirens sounded in the distance. "We've got to get out of here."

CHAPTER
THIRTY

At the northeast corner of West Thirty-Seventh, across from the Javits Center, was a high-rise construction site that Rufus was pretty sure stood on the ashes of a formerly mob-run mechanic garage and a shitty burger joint that'd had, like, at least a dozen health code violations at all times. There were no sounds of drilling or hammering, no shouting back and forth between workers. All that could be heard from the site was the ever-present wind off the Hudson whistling through the skeletal frame. Union hours must have meant work had already wrapped for the day.

Underneath the impromptu roof scaffolding, and behind the netted walkways for pedestrians, some idiot had left one of the site access doors unlocked. After a quick check both up and down the block, Rufus yanked the heavy chain from the door handles, tossed it behind a nearby Porta-Potty, and motioned Sam and Lew to follow him into the structure. Bare overhead bulbs pockmarked the site with cones of dirty yellow light, but far corners remained shrouded in harsh darkness—where even that fiery orange of a setting sun couldn't quite reach. The floor was littered with heavy machinery and various tools of the trade.

Rufus's breath came out in white plumes as he turned to face Lew. He demanded, "All right, Q-tip. What the fuck has been going on?"

"I got shot!" Lew hunched, pressing one hand against the wound in his leg. His color wasn't good, and he was shaking. "You've got to get me to a hospital!"

"Tell us what's been going on with Colonel Bridges and Del Jolly and then maybe I'll call you an ambulance," Rufus countered.

Something changed in Lew's expression—a flicker, deep in his eyes. He seemed to dismiss Rufus and turned to Sam. "I don't know what you and dipshit think you're doing, but I'm out of here."

Sam didn't answer. It looked like maybe he couldn't answer. His features were fixed, and he was breathing hard. He folded his arms and settled himself in front of the exit.

Lew threw a quick glance at Rufus again, then back to Sam. "Are you out of your fucking mind, Auden? This is kidnapping. This is false fucking imprisonment."

In the distance, the sound of the sirens was getting closer.

"Get out of the fucking way!" Lew shouted. "Do you know what kind of shit you're in?"

"Answer the question," Sam said. He didn't sound like the Sam Rufus knew. He didn't sound like anybody. "Or I'll beat you to death."

Lew's throat moved reflexively. He took a step back, his gaze swinging to Rufus again in a way that was almost a plea.

Rufus nearly missed that desperate look flicker across Lew's face because he'd been too busy staring at the stranger Sam had become. Just like that. Like a switch had been hit. Rufus licked his dry lips, tried for a deep breath, but it was like the harsh cold air couldn't reach his lungs. To Lew, he said, "I'm not kidnapping you or imprisoning you, so chill the fuck out. I want to understand what the hell is going on because people are dropping dead and I—" Rufus hesitated and then shrugged. "I just want to protect Sam. That's all."

Seconds trickled past. Then Lew laughed. He was still trying to apply pressure to the wound, and it must have hurt, but the sound wasn't amused—it was hard and ugly. "You want to protect him? Jesus, kid, that's so fucking sweet. If you want to protect him, get the fuck out of here. Like, now. Take a vacation. How does Iowa sound?" To Sam, he said, "Are you for real with this amateur hour shit?"

But Sam didn't reply.

"*Hey*," Rufus barked, and he could feel his face heating despite the cold. "I'm not a kid. I've been through enough shit in thirty-three years to make your hair turn white." Hands on his hips, Rufus said, "Answer my fucking question or you'll be *crawling* to an ambulance."

Lew shifted his weight, and pain flashed in his face. He took a calculating look at Sam, and then the tension in his body slackened, and he gave a weary shake of his head. "Someone tried to take me out," he said, the fight draining from his voice. "What the fuck does it look like?"

"Who?" Rufus demanded.

"Great question." Lew looked around and hobbled over to a crate. He eased himself against it—not quite sitting, not quite standing, but it seemed to help. The bleeding from the graze on his leg looked like it had slowed, and he closed his eyes for a moment, brow furrowed, before he opened them again. "I don't know." He must have thought Sam was going to say something because he held up his free hand and said, "Honest to God, I don't. Those two fucking train wrecks have been following me around all day, but I don't know who they are. I could have handled them if Brady hadn't pussed out."

"Stonefish," Sam said.

"Shit. I told them that bitch would find you." Lew made a face as he stretched out his leg. "Goddamn fucking Stonefish."

"It was a cover-up," Sam said. He was breathing more rapidly now. The color in his cheeks was high, but otherwise, his face looked washed out, his eyes ringed with dark circles.

"Not a very good one."

"Say it."

Lew gave him a considering look. "Nobody wanted to go down for that."

"What about Went? Did Went want to go down for it?"

In the heartbeat before it happened, Rufus realized something was about to go wrong. It was there in the way Lew paused. In the slight arch of his eyebrows. The too-smooth way he asked, "Who?"

Sam launched himself across the unfinished room.

"Sam!" Rufus threw himself into the other man's path. "*Don't.*"

"You killed him!" Sam continued to charge forward, fighting to get past Rufus. "You goddamn piece of shit, you killed him because you were too much of a fucking coward to carry your own fucking water!"

"He killed himself!" Lew shouted back. Somehow,

he'd gotten to his feet, although it was clear it was costing him. He stabbed a finger at Sam, aiming past Rufus. "That stupid pansy killed himself! It wasn't anybody's fault—it was a fucking disaster!" And then, with a child's outrage at the unfairness of it all, "Why the fuck should I take the fucking heat?"

Rufus, still shoving Sam back, the soles of his Chucks scraping against the bare concrete floor, shouted at Lew, "*Can it* with that tired, bullshit story. Sam, come on. *Sam*! If you kill him, you're no better than everyone else involved."

It took a few moments of struggle, but Sam let himself be corralled at the exit. He was panting, sweat glistening at his hairline in spite of the cold, and then he spun away from Rufus and put his hands on his knees like he might be sick.

Rufus had started after Sam, but if the painful pins and needles in his own extremities was even one percent of what his boyfriend was feeling right then, Rufus knew that touching Sam was a bad idea. He, instead, turned toward Lew. "Who were you referring to? 'That bitch would find you.'"

"Baker. That CID cunt."

"Who'd you tell that Shareed would find Sam?"

Lew shifted slightly against the crate and whispered, "Fuck." The graze might not be life threatening, but it must have hurt like hell. Or maybe Lew was just feeling the pinch of finally having his ass on the line. But he finally said, "Del. Evangeline. Colonel Bridges."

Quieter, Rufus asked, "Did you murder Colonel Bridges?"

The pause was almost nothing, but it was there. "What the fuck? Are you fucking kidding me? No. No, I did not fucking murder Colonel Bridges. What kind of half-assed op are you running here?"

Rufus crossed his arms against the cold, but it did nothing to deter the shaking and shivering that went deep, all the way past his rib cage. "You know, Lew, at the start of all this, I honestly thought Sam just had an ax to grind. I thought that maybe he hated you so much because of a past falling out that he was forcing all clues to lead back to you. But now that I've met you, I can say, with all sincerity, I wouldn't trust you to shake my dick dry. You were shit scared of Shareed contacting Sam, weren't you? Because Sam knows you. He knows you're a liar. You're a fucking liar. And a piss-poor actor, too."

"Fuck you." Lew looked past Rufus to Sam. "And fuck you. And fuck whatever this bullshit is you've got going. I didn't kill anybody, so if that's what you wanted to know, can I go to a fucking hospital now?"

"What happened to Shareed?" Sam's voice was rough, but he sounded like he was back in control of himself. "What did Del and Evangeline and the colonel say when you told them what she was going to do?"

Shaking his head, Lew said, "You don't know these people. They're insane. Look, it was one thing when—when it was an accident, all right? I mean, shit went down, but it wasn't anybody's fault. Everybody went on with their lives."

"Not everybody. Not Went."

"You know what I mean. It was fine until Shareed started poking around. Fucking junkie trying to squeeze cash out of the wrong people. Evangeline looked like a fucking ice queen, but she was psycho. She lost her mind when Shareed tried that shit. I told them to pay her off. It'd be cheaper in the long run. I told them they didn't want Shareed telling—" He didn't quite look at Sam. "—people what she'd found."

"What'd Evangeline do, Lew?"

"I don't know. I'm not saying she did anything. But

I'm telling you, you don't know these people."

"What else don't I know?"

Lew grimaced as he repositioned his hand over the wound to his leg. The drying blood made sticky noises. "You want to know who killed the colonel? How about Del fucking Jolly? Talk about a nutcase. All he cares about is his fucking company. Stonefish? Who do you think wanted to make it go away? Jesus, he would have promised anything. And then when Colonel Bridges decided he was done with Conasauga, he had a meltdown."

"And let me guess," Sam said, "you're going to try to tell me he killed Evangline too?"

"She was the one taking the colonel." Lew offered a one-shouldered shrug. "What do you think?"

Rufus waved a hand irritably, interrupting with, "How wrapped up in this is Congresswoman Nasta?"

The redirect made Lew hesitate. "Who?"

Rufus frowned a little. "Jennifer Nasta," he reiterated. "Or what about her husband—Kenny. He's a lobbyist, right?"

"Don't play dumb," Sam said.

"I mean, I heard the name…." Lew trailed off. Then he grinned—a nasty little lightning stroke that vanished almost immediately. "Shit, they dragged her into this? How?"

"That's what we want to know," Sam said.

Lew didn't respond right away, but the expression on his face suggested he was thinking. Almost absently, he said, "No clue. Sorry."

Taking a few steps toward Lew, Rufus uncrossed his arms and said, "I think you're feeding us more of that Grade A bullshit, Lew. Wanna try again?"

"Sorry, princess, I don't know. But I'd love to find out." Lew gave the unfinished building another scan. "If we're done?"

As he started to push himself up from the crate, though, he slipped, and he slid toward the floor with a pained sound. Sam stepped past Rufus—it wasn't clear if he was going to grab Lew to restrain him or to help him—and then everything went wrong.

Lew shot upright faster than should have been possible for someone who'd been clipped by a bullet. As he came up, something gleamed in his hands—a three-foot steel scaffolding support. The hollow length of metal whistled as he swung it through the air. At the last moment, Sam twisted back; reflexes saved him from being struck in the head, but the blow caught him on the arm instead, and Sam staggered back another step.

The steel support whipped toward Rufus next, and it gave Lew a temporary opening. He lurched toward the exit.

In the split second that followed the air being sliced in two, Rufus knew Lew was getting away, but he wasn't willing to lose his head over the guy, and had ducked and covered, the steel length whizzing overhead and slamming into a wall somewhere at his back. Rufus lowered his hands and looked up in time to see Lew slip out the access door. He swore, jumped to his feet, and chased after—calling for Sam, calling for Lew—and when he burst through the doorway and hurdled over the white-and-orange road barriers, he caught sight of Lew taking part in a New York moment: climbing into the back of a taxi and driving away.

CHAPTER
THIRTY-ONE

"Fucking hell," Sam said as he emerged from the construction site. The gate struck the protective fence with a crash and then wobbled halfway back.

But he was too late. Lew was gone.

Sam took a deep breath and glanced around. Dusk was deepening into dark, and above them, lights hung like mothballs, but the city was in motion again—whatever disturbance the chase and the gunshots had produced, the street outside the Javits was already subsiding into its ordinary rhythm. A few passersby startled at his sudden emergence from the construction site and circled around him, but others only gave him cursory looks, and many didn't even seem to notice. Back toward the convention center's main entrance, a couple of squad cars were parked with their lights on, and uniformed officers appeared to be taking statements.

It was harder than Sam would have liked to let go of thoughts of running out into the street, trying to spot the cab Lew had taken. He forced himself to say, "We need to get out of here."

He turned away from the squad cars and started uptown. A moment later, Rufus fell in beside him. At first, Sam walked fast—in part to get away from the police, and in part because he needed to move. The ache built in his hip, though—a reminder of his encounter with the trust fund baby in the Audi—and after the first block, he slowed. The adrenaline started to ebb; in its wake came exhaustion and a distancing numbness. They passed a litter-choked bus depot, and then the massive concrete shell of a parking garage, and then a glass tower of luxury suites. He was vaguely aware that the juxtaposition had ceased to shock him. And then he realized he'd thought of it as walking *uptown*, and not north or northeast. It was like someone turned a little valve, and the pressure went down, and he laughed, even though it didn't really feel like a laugh.

"He's full of shit," he said.

"About choking on it," Rufus said by way of agreement.

"Did you see his face when you asked him about Colonel Bridges?"

Rufus was nodding. "I thought military guys were supposed to have great poker faces."

That made Sam snort. They walked a few yards before he said, "He killed him. And he didn't plant those emails to blow Stonefish open. He left them because he didn't know the colonel had them, the dumbass."

Rufus blew a raspberry. "What're we gonna do, Sam?"

"Do you think he killed Went?" A beat of silence passed between them, and Sam struggled to break it. "He lied about the colonel. Do you think he lied about Went?"

Rufus kicked a Coke can into a pile of black-crusted snow alongside the edge of the road. He said, voice low, "I don't think my opinion means all that much. But maybe. Yeah. I've dealt with enough bad people to know when they've committed the ultimate act. It's a kind of… deadness in their eyes. Lew has dead eyes."

There was so much to say to that. So much to—to think. Instead, Sam nodded. His body carried him forward on autopilot, and they kept walking.

The cold, which he'd barely felt at first, began to settle into him. The wind picked up, gusting down the street, whipping his hair, catching up discarded flyers and empty foam cups and a flattened pack of Marlboro Reds and shoveling them down the street. Went had liked winter. He'd had a little Christmas tree, and he wasn't supposed to have that. He'd played Etta James's *12 Songs of Christmas* on his phone and let Sam listen to one of the earbuds. It hadn't been love; he loved Rufus. But he remembered the way Went's cheeks turned red in the cold.

"He didn't know about Jen," Sam said. His voice rasped, and he cleared his throat. "When you asked, it took him by surprise."

"You think so?"

"I mean, he knew who she was, but he didn't react the same way he did when you asked about the colonel." Sam checked Rufus in the pale wash of the streetlights. "What did you think?"

"Well…." Rufus let out a long, slow breath, and it was like smoke on the night. "He knows she's involved now. We said her name. But Lew was the one to suggest she'd been 'dragged into this.'"

"Right. Shit." Ahead of them, the light at the intersection changed—some jackhole in a Mercedes blazed through the red, while a guy in an old red beater tried to make the turn. They missed an accident by millimeters. Sam said,

"I guess we fucked that up. But *why* didn't he know about Jen? I mean, she's up to her nose in this shit, right? You heard her talking to Del—she had him by the balls."

"Lew might not have known about her, but what if Jen knew about Lew?" Rufus asked. "Del is the common denominator, isn't he? Lew got directions from someone. Maybe it was Del—who got them from the Congresswoman." Rufus was making a face when Sam caught his look. "Does that sound like I need to be wearing a tinfoil hat?"

"Maybe we both need tinfoil hats. Jen was definitely giving Del orders, but—I don't know. At this point, I honestly just don't know. Would she have cared about the colonel leaving Conasauga? Would she have tried to get rid of Evangeline? I mean, I just don't fucking know. But she's got something on Del—remember how he put his tail between his legs? And she didn't like that we knew something about Stonefish." Sam blew on his hands and then, in a different tone, said, "She's got something on Del, Rufus."

Rufus stopped walking. "People kill each other for a lot of stupid reasons, but mostly it's either romantic disputes or money. Sometimes that money might be twelve dollars and an old Blockbuster membership card, and other times, it might be your lobbyist husband losing millions when a competing developer takes the stage against Conasauga. But if all the biggest and brightest stars are suddenly dead…." Rufus raised his eyebrows. "No Shareed to blow a whistle on past projects gone wrong. No Evangeline to take company secrets. No colonel to take business connections."

"Kind of what I was thinking," Sam said. "Fuck. I wish we'd held on to Lew."

"Fuck Lew. I hope he's hit by a bus," Rufus replied harshly. "We don't need him. I think we should take it upon ourselves to look into Jennifer Nasta."

CHAPTER
THIRTY-TWO

Rufus was pretty savvy when it came to obtaining obscure information. Even if his childhood had not allowed for his intelligence to be properly cultivated, Rufus had kept books around starting at a young age—to keep busy, to keep loneliness at bay—and what had begun as a defense mechanism had slowly blossomed into a passion, an obsession. For knowledge, for learning about the world beyond the island of Manhattan, for stoking the fires of curiosity because the rush felt so good, and that little hit of dopamine became more precious than gold once Rufus had gotten older and depression had settled over him like an ever-present shadow. So when he'd navigated the city's massive and clunky website, and utilized the bug-ridden property records database in order to confirm Kenneth

Nasta's home address—all from his burner phone no less—Rufus wasn't surprised. He did, however, preen a little. And demand a kiss for a job well done.

Kenneth and Jennifer Nasta were homeowners in both D.C. and New York City, it turned out. In New York, they'd purchased in the neighborhood of Yorkville—tree-lined East Eighty-Ninth Street, between York Avenue and East End, if Rufus were to be a technical little shit. The town house was a gorgeous, three-story, red-brick affair, with a wrought iron gate that opened onto what constituted a front yard in Manhattan: a paved four-by-four enclosure with an empty pot beside the front door that in the summer months was probably home to some annual flower that cost more than Rufus's monthly rent.

"Guess how much they bought it for," Rufus prompted while pointing toward the home from where he and Sam stood across the street.

"A couple million?"

"Hey, you're getting pretty good at this," Rufus said, giving Sam a nudge. "Five million."

"Jesus."

"Private garages aren't free, Sam. That alone was probably a fifth of the cost." Rufus looked back at the home before saying, "Speaking of… the automatic door isn't all the way shut. See that? There's no car parked inside, though, and the lights in the house are off."

"That's convenient. What's the deal?"

Rufus shrugged. "Maybe it's malfunctioning. Kenneth should have bought a six million dollar town house instead."

"I guess so. Here we go."

Rufus waited for two cars to pass before jaywalking. He kept his hands in his jacket pockets and chin tucked against his chest, looking like any other guy just freezing his nuts off while trying to get where he needed to be that night. Rufus walked past the Nastas' garage while listening to Sam's steps closing in from behind. He listened to the scrape and scuff as Sam deviated, slipped underneath the open door, and then Rufus spun on his heel, backtracked, and hastily crouched underneath as well.

Rufus wiped road salt from his jeans before straightening his posture. Their movements activated an overhead motion-sensor light. They both stood perfectly still, listened, and only when Rufus was certain he heard nothing, did he approach the side door that accessed the home. He tried the knob but wasn't surprised to find it locked. Rufus retrieved his lockpicking tools, got down on one knee, and went to work.

It didn't take long. Not because it was a shitty lock, but because Rufus was aces at breaking and entering. He eased the door open, stared into the dark interior until his eyes adjusted, then motioned for Sam.

Sam listened at the door for a moment, but he must not have heard anything because a moment later, he pushed inside.

A long hallway opened onto an eat-in kitchen. Everything was white and stainless steel. Rufus bet that no one had ever cooked in it, let alone sat in there to share a meal. Leaving his petty thoughts behind, Rufus followed on Sam's heels, took a right out of the kitchen, and found a set of stairs. The Marash pattern of the stair runner would hide any evidence they might have tracked in on their shoes, at least to the naked eye, and so they quickly made their way to the second floor.

It was mostly what Rufus expected from a three-story town house lived in part-time by only two people: too many bedrooms and too many bathrooms. At least the Nastas hadn't fashioned all the extra space into guest rooms that'd never see any use—two of the rooms were home offices. They looked high-end in style, with built-in shelving and all-in-one printers and even those mesh trays to sort incoming and outgoing documents—which seemed unnecessary for a home office—but what the fuck did Rufus know? He didn't even file taxes.

Rufus took the first office while Sam checked the second farther down the hall. It'd turned out that Rufus scored Jennifer's room. It had also turned out that the Congresswoman had an affinity for teddy bears, which felt really creepy, given the kind of human she'd presented herself to be yesterday. Rufus counted five teddy bears placed throughout the room while he waited for the laptop on the imposing desk to power up. And when the computer sounded a little welcome jingle, the desktop loaded a wallpaper of a teddy saying: I love you bear-y much!

Rufus gagged. He navigated the Start menu, chose File Explorer, and muttered, "Let's see what Jenny's been working on of late."

A window loaded with all the recently opened files. Plenty were PDF documents with names that meant very little to Rufus—probably mundane government shit—but a few were audio files, which he found significantly more interesting. Unless Jennifer was also an audiobook junkie, why would she have that kind of stuff? Rufus double-clicked. A file was accessed on the small, external drive still plugged into the computer.

The speaker volume was low, but Rufus recognized Del's voice, speaking fast, almost babbling, really, that there wouldn't be an investigation, everything was under control because there's a sergeant taking the blame for it all.

"Holy shit." Rufus hissed, "Sam. *Sam.*" Pausing the recording, Rufus darted to the open door, poked his head into the hall, and whisper-yelled Sam's name again. "Get your ass in here."

Sam emerged from the second office, a silhouette against the ambient light, and padded down the hall.

Rufus waved him in before returning to the desk. "She's got audio recordings." He tapped Pause and Del began speaking again. "This one's the most recently played. There're lots more."

After listening for several seconds, Sam said, "He's talking about Stonefish."

Rufus was nodding. "He mentioned a sergeant taking the heat."

Sam didn't move. He didn't even seem to breathe. Finally he said, "Let me hear it."

Rufus started the recording over and let it play in its entirety.

When it stopped, Sam stared into the middle distance. Then, slowly, he nodded. He adjusted his coat—a seam bothering him, probably. One of those reflexive Sam-isms that Rufus took for granted now. Then he said, "What about the rest of them?"

"She's got them on this hard drive." Rufus tapped the drive in question before sort of blurting out, "Sam, I'm sorry."

"We knew. We already knew. It's not any different—" He stopped and scrubbed his hands over his face. When he spoke again, his voice was low and rough. "We need to listen to the others."

Rufus opened the drive and played half a dozen more recordings. They were all Del speaking. Del begging for help after Shareed contacted Evangeline, Del discussing the events that had transpired over the last few days at the Javits—events Rufus and Sam were neck-deep in—Del reporting on how the fallout surrounding Stonefish was being handled, Del incriminating Lew in the murder of Sergeant Went—

Rufus turned off the audio. He closed the file, yanked the plug from the laptop, and shoved the drive into his sweatshirt pocket before buttoning the jean jacket. "That's enough, I think," he said, glancing uneasily at Sam from the corner of his eye.

Sam still didn't seem to be seeing anything. He gave his coat another tug, and when he spoke, his voice had a stripped-down quality. "She isn't on any of them."

"But Del's talking to someone," Rufus answered. "I think we could argue he's talking to Jen, but maybe we can get Del to admit that himself. We can show him what we have—what *she* had. What do they say in those courtroom dramas: get him to flip?"

"So," Sam said, "let's get him to flip."

CHAPTER
THIRTY-THREE

Somehow, after everything that had happened, it wasn't as late as it felt. The city was quieter as Sam and Rufus made their way back toward the Savoy, but it wasn't quiet, and it wasn't still. The wind curled around buildings and seemed to be behind them no matter how many times they turned, the sound of it competing with the crunch of their footsteps. There were still cars and people, a cyclist ringing the bell on his bike as he tried to beat the light. The city that never sleeps. Sometimes, apparently, it tossed and turned in bed.

The Savoy wasn't asleep either when they got there. The lobby was full of shadows, with pools of golden light here and there to soften the darkness. An efficient-looking young woman stood at the front desk, clicking and clacking madly at one of the computers. From the bar came the clink of glasses, the swell of voices, a burst of laughter.

As Sam approached the desk, the young woman looked up at him. She put on a practiced smile and said, "Welcome to the Savoy. How may I help you?"

"I'm here to see Del Jolly. He told me to come up to his room."

"Of course. The elevators are right over there."

"The thing is," Sam said, "he forgot to tell me his room number. We met at the convention, and we were in a rush."

The woman gave him a considering once-over. Apparently, chasing a murderer on foot, being hit by a car, and then being thwacked with a metal pole gave you a certain look, because she offered the practiced smile again and said, "I'm so sorry, but we can't give out guests' private information."

Rufus interjected with "Can you give him a ring?"

"Let me see what I can do. What name should I tell him?"

"He probably won't remember my name," Sam said, "but you can tell him we met at the Stonefish panel, and I brought those papers he asked about."

More of that practiced smile. Sam tried smiling back. It didn't seem to go over well, because she turned her attention to the computer a little more quickly than was necessary and started punching keys with frantic enthusiasm. Maybe he needed a little practice himself.

After a few seconds of energetic computering, the woman picked up the phone and placed the call. Del must have picked up right away because she said, "Yes, Mr. Jolly? There are a couple of men here who'd like to see you. Yes, two of them. They said they met you at the Stonefish panel and brought some papers. Yes. Ok. Thank you, have a wonderful evening." As she returned the phone to its cradle, she beamed at Sam and said, "Room 918."

On the ride up, there was no Muzak, no piped-in environmental sounds, only the hiss of machinery: the cables and pulleys, oiled metal, air circulating in the shaft. The elevator dinged when they reached the ninth floor, and the doors slid open. 918 was to their right, three rooms from the elevator. The door was propped open—the swing lock between the door and the frame so that it couldn't close—and a DO NOT DISTURB sign hung from the handle. On the other side, the room was dark.

Rufus took off his beanie and shoved it into a pocket. Voice hardly more than a murmur, he said, "Nice to see we're being expected. I hope Del's got a mini bar because I could use a drink or four."

Sam took a deep breath and rapped on the door. The sound died away, and silence padded in after it. He took another deep breath as he worked Chad's gun out of his waistband. It was a cheap piece of shit—a Hi-Point, small enough to disappear inside Sam's grip, and it had an American flag design in black and silver on the barrel that had probably made some idiot cream his Jockeys. In theory, though, it would do the job. If it didn't stovepipe on him. Or fuck, blow up in his hand. He knocked again, but there was no answer. Nudging Rufus to the side, Sam pressed himself up against the wall and nudged the door open.

No shot. No flash. No clap of gunfire.

Instead, the light from the hall unfolded across high-traffic carpet. Sam held the door with one hand, taking in shadowy details: a desk, a sofa, a wet bar, a recliner—

The gloom made it hard to tell for sure, but Sam's mind followed the irregular bumps and knobs of shadow outlined against the recliner. It might have been something else—a blanket, maybe, or a pile of clothes. But it wasn't.

"Someone's in there," he whispered. The door seemed heavier than it should have been, and he fought the urge to drop his hand and let it swing shut. "A body. In the chair."

"*What*?" Rufus hissed. "Who? Can you see?"

Sam shook his head. He checked the hallway; they were still alone, but not for long. He reached through the doorway with the hand holding the gun, found the light switch just inside the room, and flipped it. A single overhead light came on immediately inside the room.

Still nothing. No one burst out of hiding. No one fired.

It was enough light to make out Del's face in profile. The entry wound from the bullet looked small, almost clean, on the side of his head—at that distance, like a little black circle. The other side, where it had exited, would be a lot worse.

"Stay here," Sam whispered and stepped into the room.

"Like fuck." Rufus's counter was barely audible. He slipped into the room behind Sam.

Sam flipped the swing lock out of the way and let the door close. It settled into its frame with a click. Now Sam could smell it—piss, blood, what he thought was a lingering whiff of gunfire. They would have killed him here; it would have been too much trouble to maneuver a corpse through the Savoy. It had probably happened not long after Sam and Rufus got away from Chad and Shane the day before.

As Sam moved across the room toward Del's body, he was vaguely aware of Rufus splitting off toward the bathroom. The thud of Sam's pulse wasn't really a sound, but it kept time for the whisper of the room's HVAC system, and the hoarse rattle of the wind wrapping itself around the building, subsiding, and picking up again. Del already had that shrunken look that people took on after death. A hint of gray stubble showed on one flaccid cheek. Rigor had come and gone, but one hand was still curled into a claw, and his big, expensive watch had slid on his wrist and was now upside down. When they'd dragged him over there. When they'd hauled him into the chair like a sack of meat.

The smell was starting to get into Sam's nose, settle there. It stung his nostrils—that was the body's way of telling him to get the fuck out of here—and it made the hair on the back of his neck bristle. He tried breathing through his mouth, but it wasn't much better.

Del was dead.

Colonel Bridges was dead.

Evangeline was dead.

Nobody was going to flip on Jen Nasta. Nobody was going to talk. The recordings weren't worth shit.

He heard himself breathing through his mouth, the plosive bursts of it. He stared at the blackout curtains. If you pulled them open, there'd be eight million people pressed up against the fucking glass.

Went was still dead.

A soft sound suggested Rufus had come up behind him. Sam said, "Let's go."

But when he turned around, it wasn't Rufus. It was Lew.

Lew looked even worse than he had earlier that evening. The scrapes and scratches on his face had stopped bleeding, and now they had that raw, inflamed look of a wound before it scabbed. A drying line of rust-colored flakes snaked down the side of his neck to stain his shirt. He'd fixed some kind of impromptu bandage where the bullet had caught him, but it was over his jeans, and it looked like the graze was still seeping. Sam's first, disjointed thought was that he couldn't believe they'd let him in the Savoy looking like that. But in one hand, Lew held a compact pistol, the gun aimed at Sam's chest. So maybe that had something to do with it.

"Drop it," Lew said.

Sam tried to take a slower, deeper breath, but he couldn't. The air kept exploding from his lungs.

"Drop the fucking gun," Lew said.

"You killed Went," Sam said. His mouth was cottony. Anesthetized. He had the strange sense that he was falling.

"Fucking pathetic little cocksucking fuck. He was crying when I got there. He wanted a hug. The little faggot tried to kiss me." He ran his free hand across his mouth—unconsciously, maybe. Or maybe not. Went had always thought he had a beautiful mouth. "I did him a favor. Now drop the gun."

Sam noticed the slightest movement over Lew's shoulder—Rufus crept on the worn-out soles of his shoes toward the open closet, silently reaching for the iron mounted to the wall beside the accompanying board.

"We heard the recordings. She's got Del talking about all of it."

"I'll shoot you right here if I have to. Or we can do this nice and easy, Sam. It'll be over fast."

Sam didn't say anything. He tried to swallow, but his throat was too tight. He knew he should be thinking about the gun. He knew he should be focused on the gun. But his brain kept strobing. Went loading up on mashed potatoes in the chow. Went freaking out because he'd walked through poison sumac to take a leak. And that final night, his brain building the image out of bits and pieces: Went alone in the barracks. Until Lew showed up.

He'd been a kid. And Sam had promised himself he'd watch out for him.

Maybe Lew felt it, the change, the decision. His own expression hardened.

Rufus had unhooked the iron without making a sound.

In the same split second that Lew's grip on the pistol tightened, Rufus swung the iron against the back of Lew's head.

As Lew stumbled, Sam launched himself forward. He brought the cheap little pistol up and then hammered down on the side of Lew's head with it. The force of the blow redirected Lew sideways, and he hit the coffee table. His gun went off—for an instant, the muzzle flash was blinding, and then Sam's ears rang from the sound of the shot. The stink of gunpowder filled Sam's nose. Blinking to clear his vision, he closed with Lew again. The other man was trying to push himself up from the table, but between the blows to the head and his injured leg, he was having a hard time. Sam kicked Lew's hand and felt something— one of the tiny bones there—give. Somehow, Lew held on to the gun. He got off another shot. The muzzle flash dazzled Sam again, and then, in the darkness that swept in, the afterimage floated in front of him. He grabbed Lew by the arm and dragged him off the table, riding him down to the floor. They landed hard, the jolt zinging up to Sam's hip. He slammed Lew's hand against the floor once, and then he yanked the gun free. He felt Lew's index finger snap when it caught in the trigger guard.

Scrambling to his feet, Sam aimed the piece-of-shit pistol at Lew. He couldn't breathe. He couldn't hear—the sound of the gunshot was like a bell being rung inside his head. He felt like he was on fire.

From a long way off, Lew was shouting, "Don't! Don't! Don't! We can make a deal! I'll tell you about Del, about Stonefish—" Panic sharpened his voice. "I'll talk!"

Sam's hand trembled. The gun dipped, floated, centered on Lew again. His finger tightened on the trigger.

Rufus grabbed Sam's shoulder. "Sam, come on, please don't. This piece of shit isn't worth your life. If you shoot him you'll be in prison until you're dead. Please."

It was like pushing something that was too heavy, almost impossibly heavy. Like trying to move a boulder. And that distant part of himself recognized that yes, it was like that, because this had been a weight on him, crushing him, for a long time. So long that, some days, he wasn't even aware of it anymore.

And then, slowly, it began to shift. His chest hitched. His breathing came thin and high. He wanted to close his eyes or cry or both. But he didn't. He fumbled the pistol toward Rufus and dried his hands on his jeans and limped away.

CHAPTER
THIRTY-FOUR

Rufus knew he was being hypocritical.

He lived off of greasy pizza, diner pancakes, expired bodega snacks, and cheap alcohol he "borrowed" from Pauly Paul. His palate was underdeveloped and he'd probably die of heart disease before he hit fifty. But all that being said, police precinct coffee was fucking terrible.

It was brewed too strong, left on the burner for too long, and the only sugar the motherfuckers had were packs of Splenda.

He drank it anyway.

Rufus had been in an interview room at One Police Plaza—referred to by cops, crooks, and informants alike as 1PP—since last night, and he had no intention of falling asleep around a bunch of police he didn't trust, but mostly, he drank the shitty coffee because he was bored. Rufus took one last swig before making a face. At least the cup was mostly empty now. He started picking the Styrofoam apart.

The door opened, sending a current of stale air wafting through the room, and Erik stepped inside. The dark eyes, the loosened tie, the rumpled clothes—he'd been up all night too. And he didn't look happy about it.

"What the fuck," he asked as he dropped into the seat opposite Rufus, "were you thinking?"

Rufus brushed the bits of Styrofoam to the floor while saying, "You'll have to be more specific."

Erik breathed through his nose. Then he slapped the cup—what was left of it—and sent it flying across the room, with a little comet tail of coffee trailing behind it. In the silence, the sound of the coffee spattering the floor was loud. "Start talking. And don't leave out any of it."

Rufus absently wiped his hands. Then he pulled free the black hard drive he'd swiped from Jen's home office. He didn't pass it over, instead clutched it tight to his chest. "Would you say I'm pretty levelheaded? Seriously, Erik. I might annoy you, but I'm not insane, right?"

"There's a string of dead bodies leading to you in a hotel room with another dead guy. I'd say the jury is still out."

"Oh no, they don't lead to me. I got tangled up in all this because the powers that be tried to drag *Sam* into it. How does conspiracy to commit murder sound to you?"

"It sounds like a lot of fucking paperwork." But some of the anger seemed to have leached out of him, and he said, "Do you have something? Besides that guy? Because I'm telling you, as soon as he lawyers up, he's going to walk it all back. For Christ's sake, you were holding a gun on him."

"*I* was holding an iron on him," Rufus corrected. He smiled a little and said with a false bravado, "Never even used one before." But when Erik didn't laugh, Rufus said, "Ok. As far as I understand it all, there was some Army mishap years ago called Stonefish. Soldiers died. A guy named Sergeant Went took the blame, but Sam has always insisted he was killed—murdered—and it was all a government cover-up. I thought it was bullshit in the beginning. I fully admit to not believing Sam. But then a whistleblower—Shareed Baker—was found dead.

"We went to the MoDe conference at the Javits where Conasauga was in attendance. They have contracts with the Army and were involved with the Stonefish project. You're thinking, maybe that's a coincidence, right? Except insider gossip at the conference was that Evangeline Ridgeway, the company's golden goose, was leaving to work for a competing firm—New Haven—and she was taking big-time military contacts with her. Like Colonel Bridges. But guess what? They both wound up dead this week. And if *that's* not totally fucking wild enough for you, I've got some recordings on this hard drive that paint Del Jolly of Conasauga in some very bad light. He did business with lobbyist Kenneth Nasta—the husband of Jennifer Nasta." Rufus reluctantly set the hard drive on the tabletop. "That's who you need to look at, Erik. She didn't commit the murders, but she's been pulling Del's strings. *He* was pulling Lew's. She made them kill those people—Shareed, Evangeline, Colonel Bridges."

Erik leaned back in his seat. After several seconds, he asked, "Who the hell is Jennifer Nasta?"

"A Congresswoman," Rufus replied. "She's on the Defense Subcommittee."

"Fuck me."

Rufus didn't take the easy route with a joke. He just didn't feel like joking anymore. "Lew leads to Del, Del leads to Jennifer, and Jennifer's protecting her cashflow." Rufus began ticking off more names on his fingers. "Brady Ellsworth, Chad Deangelis—that coke dealer—some guy calling himself Shane. This goes deep, Erik." Rufus tapped the hard drive while saying, "And this isn't over. You have to listen to these recordings. *Swear* you'll listen?"

"Most CIs bring me a gangbanger, you know. They don't drop a fucking congresswoman in my lap."

"These people tried to kill me," Rufus said. "They tried to kill Sam. They *did* kill several people—in the NYPD's own backyard. Look, I'll… I'll even testify in court. I'm that serious about what's going on."

Erik grunted. "We'll see about that. I want to hear what's on that drive first."

Rufus nodded. He pushed back his chair but didn't stand. "Sam isn't under arrest, is he? It was self-defense, you know. Lew was going to shoot him first."

"That," Erik said as he dragged the hard drive toward him, "is literally the least of my worries."

CHAPTER
THIRTY-FIVE

Eventually, they were allowed to go home. After being awake for over twenty-four hours, and with nothing but bad coffee in him for the last twelve, Sam was barely conscious for the taxi ride. He was vaguely aware of the last staggering steps toward Rufus's bed, yanking off his boots, and collapsing—fully clothed—onto the mattress. The last thought that ballooned up to him out of the darkness was that he hadn't thought of it as Rufus's apartment. He had thought, *Home*.

He woke to the sounds—and light—of the city in late morning. Horns, engines, the grinding restlessness of machines and people that never stopped moving. His head was pounding, his hip was killing him, and he was aware of every sticky, grimy inch of himself in a way that was already working itself up into a need. To shower, at the minimum. Rufus snored next to him; the redhead was bare chested, still in his jeans and Chucks. The elastic band of his underwear had ridden up the small of his back.

After stripping off his clothes, Sam found clean ones in the ruck. He got his soap. The studio was too small for a dresser, he thought, but he'd seen plastic things you could slide under the bed. He drank water from the sink as he waited for the shower to warm up. Palpated his hip. A tote, he thought. That's what they were called.

The water never really got hot, but when it was bearable, he got under the spray. He washed slowly—as much because of all the aches and bruises as because he enjoyed the feeling of the water sluicing away the sweat and dirt. A real Christmas tree wouldn't fit, but they could find one of the tiny ones, the kind that could sit on a desk. Like Went's. And then he remembered it was after Christmas. And Went was still dead. He had thought, somehow, it would feel different. Maybe it would, eventually. He turned his face into the spray until the need to breathe was big enough to drive out everything else in his head.

When he left the bathroom, Rufus was sitting up in bed.

"Morning," Sam said as he dried himself.

"Morning," Rufus managed around a yawn. "Why're you up already?"

"Couldn't sleep. Why're you up?"

"Because you are."

"That's a pretty good reason. I was going to get us something to eat. Do you want anything in particular?"

Rufus looked out the window before saying, "BlueMoon?"

So, after Rufus had showered and dressed, they took a cab to BlueMoon. They managed to hit it at the sweet spot between breakfast and lunch, which meant Maddie shooed them toward a booth and brought them coffee before they'd finished sitting down.

"You look like a train ran over you."

"Thanks," Sam said.

"You're just saying that," Rufus said, mock-batting his eyelashes.

Maddie's look came straight out of the mom handbook—from the *disappointed* section, Sam thought—but she took their orders without further commentary and moved on to the next table.

"So," Sam said and picked up one of the packets of creamer. He toyed with the little tab on the top. "I was thinking."

"Uh-oh. I'm the one who does too much of that." Rufus shook a sugar packet into his hand.

"Yeah, well." Sam tried for a laugh, but it didn't quite land. "Guess it's catching." The silence after that was almost enough to make him stumble, and he stumbled to add, "I've been thinking about us, I mean. About what we're going to do."

Rufus stared at Sam for a long moment. He dumped the sugar onto the tabletop, wiped his hands, and leaned forward. "If you're leaving or dumping me or—rip the Band-Aid fast, won't you?"

The little plastic tab tore, and creamer spilled over Sam's hands. Swearing, he grabbed napkins. "What? Rufus, what—we literally just talked about this. I love you. I'm not breaking up with you." And then it happened—he blurted, "I think I'm going to go to college."

Rufus's eyebrows rose. The sharp edge of his shoulders softened. "Oh. Ok. I mean, I think that's really cool, actually."

"Yeah?" That broken-off laugh slipped out of him

again. "I don't know. I mean, I'm not exactly going to blend in. I'm way too old, and—" He stopped and managed to say again, "I don't know. I guess we'll see. I need to figure out what I want to do first. And, you know, where. I've got the GI bill, so there's that. And I've still got some money put away."

Rufus was smiling now. "I've heard the community and city colleges are actually pretty good. I bet you can find classes for anything you're interested in."

"Yeah." Sam snapped the paper band on the bundle of flatware. "I guess I was thinking, you know, maybe we could both do it. Try some classes, I mean. If you want to. I know you don't need to go to school. You're so smart, and you already learn whatever you want—"

Rufus's complexion was taking on color. Not embarrassment, Sam realized, but upset. It made his freckles pop out. Rufus said, "I don't think high school dropouts are allowed to go to college."

"Oh. Yeah, I don't know. But you could take the test, right? Get your GED?"

"I—I mean… maybe. I never really thought about it before." Rufus wiped his eyes on the sleeve of his shirt. He seemed to be seriously considering the suggestion.

"You wouldn't even need to study for it, I bet. And I know college is expensive, but there are grants, scholarships. We could look at loans. We can't live on what I've got saved forever, but we could figure out something. We could make it work." Sam reached across the table and took Rufus's hand. He looked him in the eye. He smiled, surprised, after everything that happened, that he could still feel so nervous. And, also, kind of loving it. "We can do this," he said. "Let's do this."

Sam Auden and Rufus O'Callaghan return in:

A Friend in the Wind
(An Auden & O'Callaghan Mystery: Book Four)

Gregory Ashe is a longtime Midwesterner. He has lived in Chicago, Bloomington (IN), and Saint Louis, his current home. When not reading and writing (which take up a lot of his time), he is an educator.

gregoryashe.com

ALSO BY GREGORY ASHE

SERIES:
The Hazard and Somerset Mysteries
Hazard and Somerset: A Union of Swords
Hazard and Somerset: Arrows in the Hand
Iron on Iron
Hazardverse: Sidetracks
The Borealis Investigations
Borealis: Without a Compass
The First Quarto
The Lamb and the Lion
The Last Picks
Luka Meer
The Adventures of Holloway Holmes
Hollow Folk
Flint and Tinder
The DuPage Parish Mysteries
An Auden & O'Callaghan Mystery
(co-written with C.S. Poe)

Join Gregory Ashe's mailing list for advanced access,
exclusive content, limited-time promotions, and insider
information.
bit.ly/ashemailinglist

C.S. Poe is an author of gay mystery, romance, and speculative fiction. She is a winner of the FAPA, Next Generation, and e-Lit book awards, as well as a finalist of the Lambda Literary and EPIC awards.

She resides in New York City, but has also called Key West and Ibaraki, Japan, home. She's a Gilded Age New York historian, loves Romanticism artwork, the films of Buster Keaton, coffee in the morning and whiskey in the evening, true crime, and cats. She's rescued two cats—Milo and Kasper do their best to distract her from work on a daily basis.

C.S. is an alumna of the School of Visual Arts.

Her debut novel, *The Mystery of Nevermore*, was published 2016.

cspoe.com

ALSO BY C.S. POE

SERIES:
Snow & Winter
Snow & Winter Collection
Magic & Steam
A Lancaster Story
The Silver Screen
Memento Mori
An Auden & O'Callaghan Mystery
(co-written with Gregory Ashe)

NOVELS:
Southernmost Murder

NOVELLAS:
11:59

SHORT STORIES:
Curio
Love in 24 Frames
That Turtle Story
New Game, Start
Love Has No Expiration

Visit **cspoe.com** for the latest book and audio releases,
as well as available translations.

Join C.S. Poe's newsletter for information on upcoming
projects, read advance excerpts and free flash fiction, stay
up-to-date on sales, conference appearances,
and much more!
https://bit.ly/CSPoeNewsletter

Follow C.S. Poe on Goodreads to keep your books
organized and reviewed and BookBub to be the first
notified of new releases and sales!

Check out C.S. Poe's social media links:
https://linktr.ee/cspoe